The King and the Storyteller

Dear Andy and Beth,

Alfie, Indigo and Jacob

with love and thanks -

Anthony

Anthony Buckley

Christmas,

2015

New Generation Publishing

Dedication

To my parents, who developed my love of reading and thus of stories.

To Monica, Frances and Richard, who needed to be very patient.

And to Felicity, whose kind encouragement never faltered.

Contents

Chapter 1: The library and the advertisement

Mark Lind liked the local library. He liked being surrounded by books. He liked being in the unspoken company of others who liked books. He liked it that everyone in a library had a purpose. To read, borrow or return. To occupy the children. To be out of the rain, to doze in the warm. Whatever the reason, people had chosen to be there.

Fridays held an extra attraction, this was when the teaching vacancies were published. He would go upstairs where the large wooden desks were placed, spread out the paper and scan the lists.

He had walked leisurely towards the library that morning, the third Friday in September, and was now settled in his usual place on the first floor.

He read the advertisement again. He had not been in regular work since Christmas; a little supply teaching had come his way but schools were watching their budgets and he was seldom offered more than one day at a time.

He read the advertisement a third time.

Why do throwaway lines have such a powerful effect? The night before he had been out with friends. They had touched on all sorts of issues, conversation slowing and quickening as new topics were found. Mark had enjoyed it. He knew his friends were more intelligent and usually better informed than he was; he relished being part of the discussions, occasionally chipping in but knowing enough not to look foolish by saying too much.

He remembered little of last night's wisdom expounded on the state of the government, the significance of a recent scientific advance or the surprising new interpretation of the causes of inflation. But he did remember Henry leaning forward with a triumphant smile: "There, I told you, no one tells stories like Mark!" It was an off-hand remark, in response to a brief and unimportant anecdote Mark had told about a man he had met at a bus station.

No one tells stories like Mark. The sentence stuck in his mind. He did not feel he did anything especially well and here was Henry (Henry!) praising him in front of the others. He would not have dared relive this moment to anyone else; that would have sounded much too boastful. He knew that it was only a passing thought and Henry had meant nothing by it. But Mark would keep and protect it. Such moments were important to him.

People had taken Mark aside over the years. They had hinted that his potential was not quite being fulfilled and had suggested training or a change of career. He had wondered about applying for different jobs but then realised that they were out of his reach. He quite enjoyed being a supply teacher but was sometimes frustrated by not feeling fully part of a school. Enough money came in for the rent on his flat and the necessities. He lived on his own and his material desires were few. Most of the time he was content and could keep the advice-givers at bay.

No one tells stories like Mark. Henry's comment was still in Mark's mind that Friday morning. He usually had no need of his small notebook and pen but today he did. He reached behind and retrieved them from the pocket of his coat, hanging over the back of his chair. He began to copy the details.

Why do throwaway lines have such an effect? Perhaps it was simply the timing, thought Mark, a comment one night, an advertisement the next day. Perhaps there is nothing significant in this after all. Are we in a dance or are we in chaos?

Mark Lind had heard of the school, of course. Probably most people scattered around the library that September day, choosing books, resting, returning books, browsing shelves, had heard of the school.

But he had never heard of such a post before.

St. George's. Storyteller and poet required. Full-time.

Chapter 2: The interview and the story

Two weeks later he was sitting in the Headmaster's study.

"You were the only serious applicant," Mr English was saying, facing him across a large circular desk that seemed to fill most of the room. He smiled. "Do you think our country is lacking storytellers? Have we gone short of poets? No, don't worry about answering. And I know you see yourself as a storyteller, not as a poet. In truth, there were some applications, but we wanted someone who would fit with what we are. You came closest and that is why you are the only one being interviewed today."

His voice became more business-like. "Now, imagine it is ten minutes before the end of a lesson on a Friday afternoon. A teacher has to leave her class. She sends a message for you to come and tell them a story. They are a normal mix of happy, unconcerned, keen, tired, untidy twelve- and thirteen-year-olds. What would you say? Tell me the story you would give them."

Mark was nonplussed. He had been expecting a question about his last post, or his previous experience. "I am not sure I have got anything exactly ready…"

"I know that. I want to see what you would do on the spur of the moment." The Headmaster leaned back in his chair and closed his eyes.

"Sir Richard was standing looking over the battlements from the tallest turret of his castle." began Mark hesitantly, and then paused.

The eyes slowly opened, looked expectantly across the table, and then closed again.

Mark began again.

"Sir Richard was standing looking over the battlements from the tallest turret of his castle. He had not climbed the one hundred and thirty-three steps to look at anything in particular. He was there because he wanted to think and he wanted to talk, and this was the place in the castle where he was least likely to be disturbed.

He was a 'Miril'. A leading knight of the realm. Someone who had proved his courage, loyalty and honour many times. Many years earlier, a king who spoke Latin (but not very well) used to say that a successful knight was 'mirabilis' – marvellous. Succeeding kings had taken up the idea. 'Mirabilis' became shortened to 'Miril' and it became a title of honour. There were nine Mirils at a time, echoing the nine heroes of ancient stories. The king would only appoint a new one only if an old one died.

Sir Richard wanted to think and he wanted to talk. With him on the turret was a lady called Catherine. She had brought news to him that morning. He had listened carefully, asked one or two questions, and said he needed time to consider what to do. They had agreed to talk again, and this was the meeting time.

"So he is on his way," Sir Richard said calmly.

"Not directly approaching you. He would not dare. But he is occupying everything from the mountains to the river. He challenges the authority of the king, he is setting up his own courts and claiming taxes for himself. The people are confused and worried, the king is far away. Richard, will you go? You are needed. Have you decided? Will you go out with your men and fight?"

"Will I go and fight?" repeated the knight thoughtfully. "I sometimes feel old – No," he said with a smile, as he saw Catherine about to protest. "I do not mean I am not strong enough. I am not being falsely modest. I know that I have the power and I have the men. But I am old enough to want to pause.

"When I fight wars, people suffer. Not only my enemies, but ordinary people, whose only crime is that they are in the wrong place when two over-proud knights want to throw their weight around."

"You are wrong to compare yourself with him. You are different. You are a man of honour. You are a Miril."

"Yes, and that gives me the right to pause. Does it really matter to the farmers and the villagers which knight holds sway? I can unleash war once more. But who pays the price? People caught up in events bigger than themselves."

He turned from the view and smiled at Catherine. "One last time. One last time. Is that what you are saying? The armour buckled on once more, the plans made, the campaign beginning. The old man rides again. One last time to face the battle?"

"Perhaps it matters more to the farmers and the villagers than you think it does," said Catherine and then was silent. They smiled at each other, Richard took her hand in his.

"You are who you are," Catherine said quietly. "You are what you are called to be."

Mark stopped.

Mr English opened his eyes and looked inquiringly.

"That's where I would leave it," said Mark.

"Would you always leave a story hanging like that?"

"I was thinking that I need to hold them for that last ten minutes of that lesson. I might tell the story for the first five and then ask them to continue it as they think best. And also, to be honest, I am not quite sure which way I would go myself."

"Being unsure of where it will go is no reason to stop telling a story," said Mr English. "But I liked the uncertainties – who are these mysterious 'Mirils'? And the sense of deep soil in 'echoing the nine old heroes'. And we wonder what the relationship is between the two characters? And of course, the central issue: is he going to fight? The suffering of the vulnerable and the bystander weighed against the need to do what is right.

"One or two of the words you used would be difficult for some of the pupils to grasp. I like that. They like that too. Children like being stretched, to feel they are entering a world just beyond their own. I am not sure about asking them to continue it themselves. You are the storyteller. They want to lose themselves in it, not have to do a task."

Mr English paused. He looked thoughtfully at Mark, then continued: "Now, perhaps a more difficult one. You can tell a story. Can you also be a poet? You say that this is not your strength, but I need to hear you try. I will leave you for five minutes. Will that be long enough for you to write a poem relating to that story?" He pushed a pad of paper across the table.

Mark nodded. "I'll have a try." This, he thought, was becoming the most extraordinary interview he had ever had. He picked up his notepad and stared at the blank paper.

When the Headmaster returned he brought with him two pupils. "Allow me to introduce Issie and Jane. I have told them, as best I can, the story you told me. They have come to hear your poem." The girls, aged about fifteen or sixteen, Mark guessed, were ushered to chairs round the desk. He began to read:

Rest your eyes on quiet fields, as gentle falls the day
Watch the home-bound traveller, who walks along the lane
Hear the evening sounds, of farms and homes and sky
Feel the air, fresh with Spring, full of promised life

Rest your eyes on distant hills, where ancient woods still sway
Watch the children dance and run, who change from school to play
Hear the shouts and laughter, the freedom that is theirs
Feel the air, fresh with Spring, full of promised life

Just once, just once, I beg you think, whether the cost is right
The enemy must be fought, you say, but who will pay the price?
Is this the only way to win, are no other words to hand?
Feel the air, heavy with life, hear the promised Spring!

***

I say to you there comes a time
When for a noble cause
It's right to fight, it's right to win
And there's no time to pause.

If your army stays at home, then others will appear
And they will mar and they will end your treasured village peace

You have the strength to keep it safe, to let the children play.
If you refuse to make the move, the Spring will fade and die.

He stopped.

Mr English looked enquiringly at the pupils.

"I wasn't sure about the phrase 'To make the move'," said Issie. "But apart from that I thought the whole thing was really good."

"Jane?" asked the Headmaster.

"I couldn't work out whether it was rhyming or not, and the change of tone meant it was quite difficult to follow, but I think I liked it."

There was a pause. Then Issie asked: "Mr English, what did you think of it?"

"What I liked," said the Headmaster, "was that Mr Lind did his best." He smiled.

"Mr Lind, I am offering you the post of storyteller and poet. Will you accept?"

A hundred questions raced through Mark's mind. He had not been shown the school. He had not faced the usual demands of an interview. How much did they know about him? How much did he know about them? All he had done was tell the beginning of a story and hurriedly write a poem (and he was very conscious of the inadequacies of both story and poem). But it was a job, and he needed a job. How could a school afford a salary for a post like this when so many schools were struggling to fill normal teaching posts? He looked at Mr English and sensed that the Headmaster understood his mix of emotions and uncertainties, that he was being asked to make a decision based on instinct and trust, that this was about relationships as much as a role to fill. He looked at the students. What sort of school is this when they are still present when a job offer is being made?

"I accept."

Mr English's smile grew broader and he got to his feet. Jane and Issie stood. It felt a strangely theatrical or even ceremonial moment and Mark felt he should likewise stand. Mark fleetingly felt or imagined an ancient, distant, echo of something he did not understand. The moment suddenly seemed rather significant.

"Thank you," said the Headmaster. "On behalf of all of us, thank you."

Chapter 3: Kings and power, poems and words

"If you don't mind me asking, Mr English, how can the school afford my post?"

It was Monday of the next week and Mark was sitting again in the Headmaster's study. This was his first full day. Over the weekend all the more usual questions surrounding a new job had come back to mind and he was determined to ask as many as he could.

"The arrangements for St. George's are quite complex," Mr English explained. "As well as government funding we receive some money from historic trusts and some kind wealthy individuals. One of these individuals agreed over the summer that this post was needed at this time at this school. That person is providing the money."

"Will I meet him?"

"Did I say it was a 'him'? I expect you will." replied the Headmaster.

"Now, I know you will have many practical questions and as time goes by we will find time to answer them as best we can, but this morning I think we need to get you visible round the school. We are already in the sixth week of term. Everyone else is settled in and you will be feeling and appearing very new. The sooner you are out and about the better. The story you told at your interview shows you like history and I think that was your original subject? No doubt you like other things as well, but this morning I will take you to a history lesson. You can spend time there and then meet the rest of the teachers at break in the staff room."

Mr English accompanied Mark down a corridor, knocked on a door and went in. The students stood up politely.

"Dr Edwards and enthusiastic historians. May I introduce Mr Lind? He would like to sit in on your class for the lesson. He is the first holder of a new post: 'Storyteller and Poet'. That's rather a mouthful. If anyone can think of a snappier title, please tell me before the end of the day. We can't call him 'STAP' – that really does not work. Better suggestions please, do come and find me if you have one." The Headmaster smiled, bowed slightly and went out.

Dr Edwards motioned the pupils to sit.

"It is a pleasure for us to have Mr Lind with us. Mr Lind, in ten minutes would you be kind enough to give us some riddle poems about historical events or people?"

I am going to have to get used to this, thought Mark.

"I would be pleased to," he said, trying to look more relaxed than he felt, and went to an empty chair near the back. He pulled out his notebook and began to think.

The pupils continued to work. After a few minutes the teacher looked over. "Ready?" he mouthed. Mark nodded. He walked to the front of the class.

"Good morning everyone. As you know, I am new to the school and you are the first class that I have met. Here are some short poems. I will pause after each one and you can tell me if you know what person they are meant to be about. Here is the first."

Alone, hard-pressed, retreating, the tired king lacks all.
Hoped-for risings failed, replaced with fall on fall
The enemy is gaining ground, with triumph in his eyes
If royal light is crushed to dust, the hope of England dies

Forget the songs and minstrel tales, forget the later myths
Forget it if the cakes are burned, forget all else but this
It all comes back to holding on, re-grouping once for all
In the silence of the lonely hour, will he stand or fall?

Hands shot up.

"Er – you at the back," said Mark.

"Is it Alfred the Great?"

"Well done, James." interjected Dr Edwards, "How could you tell?"

"It was the cakes."

"Well done," said Mark. "Here's another."

A cold morning, a dry morning, a journey ending here.
Manipulating traitor or sacrificial King?
Martyr saint or tyrant fool? – different voices say.
Double-wrapped against the cold, no shivering today.

The crowd is pale and deathly quiet, we've not done this before.
Iconoclastic regicide or Englishman supreme?
The steady eyes are looking on, hand never far from sword.
Sometimes faith needs weapons, if you're fighting for the Lord.

This time there was no response.

"This may be a little out of our range," said Dr Edwards. "We will do the Stuarts later this year, I am not going to give the answer now. And we might need to expand our vocabulary somewhat. We will ask Mr Lind to join us again when we get to that point in the syllabus." He turned to Mark. "Perhaps one more from the Middle Ages?"

Mark thought hard for a few seconds and then spoke:

I nod and smile and stamp the seal, but my mind is far away
Mocking these poor barons who think they have their day
This silly scrap of paper will be ripped and burnt and lost
And my power will rise triumphant, whatever be the cost.

"Magna Carta, Magna Carta," the voices called. Dr Edwards turned to Mark and nodded. "Thank you for being with us, we enjoyed it. And congratulations, class, you did well. Mr Lind will need to go now but we will give some time to thinking about what themes connected his poems. An interesting choice of topics indeed." The pupils smiled politely and Mark left the room.

Mark made his way to the staff room. It was still fifteen minutes until break and he thought he would relax until others appeared. When he arrived he saw that someone was already there.

"Good morning, you must be Mark Lind. My name is Jennifer Loss, people call me Jenny. Been here a very long time, teach English, and always glad to see a new face. How are you settling in?"

"It all feels very new and like nothing I've done before. It seems that my role is to be a kind of minstrel without the music! I've just been in a history class, making up poems. Is that what people think I should be doing?"

"When the Head told us the plan to create such a role, this was more or less the picture. But of course none of us quite know what it will look like. Don't underestimate what you are doing. You will be expressing and interpreting what is going on in a different way to the rest of us. Imagine you are a court jester in a mediaeval court. You have no power or authority but you have the freedom to speak truth. Don't worry, you are not expected to be constantly funny, like a film version of a jester, which was never their most important role. We hope you will be able to help people see things from a different angle and perhaps therefore more clearly. Let me give you an example: I am a form tutor and spend a lot of time with pupils and parents. Sometimes the things I am told affect me quite deeply. Can you give me a poem that sums up what I may be feeling?"

"Five minutes?" said Mark, again feeling somewhat put on the spot.

"Whatever you need."

Mark retreated to the other end of the room. In a few minutes he returned to where Jenny was sitting.

"It's not very good, but here goes."

Before he could begin, she broke in, "It is important that you do not apologise before you deliver the poem or the story you are asked for. Those who ask will probably already know the constraints you are under. Be yourself and do what you can." Her voice softened. "Sorry about being blunt, that's the teacher in me. Let's hear it now."

Mark nodded. He had indeed been slightly taken aback by her directness, asking for a poem on first meeting, correcting him a few moments later. But there was a thrill to it all. His creativity, and he himself, were being taken seriously, and he liked that. He read from his notepad:

If you say that to me then perhaps I will cry
Yes, partly for you, for the hurt in your eyes
But also for me, for the echoes you bring

You are bright and will know that I looked away then
You saw my eyes glisten and a pause in my voice
You wondered perhaps, but then ever polite
You let me say more about you than of me

I was and am you. I sat where you sit
Living the pain and lost by events
When the map makes no sense and the signposts are gone

And so you help me and perhaps I help you
We stumble together, young and old, through all this
And I will fade from your mind as another day dawns.

Jenny said nothing for a few moments. She looked up at Mark.

"You have an interesting gift. Use it well. I know why it was felt we needed someone like you." The bell went somewhere in the corridor. "They're coming in. Go and get yourself a coffee and we'll see who turns up."

* * *

"Mr Lind?"

"Yes, but do call me Mark."

"Ed Moore. I teach Geography."

Mark had collected his coffee from the counter and was now sitting in one of the assorted colourful chairs dotted round the room. Ed Moore sat next to him. "Welcome to the school. I hope you'll get on well."

"Thank you. I've just been in a history lesson with Dr Edwards."

"Ah yes, dear old Frank. Well. I am sure that went fine. Done much of this stuff before?"

"No, to be honest. It all feels a bit new to me. Producing poems and stories on demand."

"Well, yes. I'll be honest with you, too. Not everyone can see why English wanted you here. Not you, personally, of course, great to have you here; it is the role we are not sure about. I am sure you will do your best to fit in and it won't be a distraction to the real work, but you can perhaps see that it feels a little unusual?"

"I will try to help, rather than hinder," said Mark, conscious that his nervousness was causing him to speak rather stiffly, "but I am aware that I am finding my way. I'll always be grateful for any guidance."

"I am sure you will. As you can see, I always like to tell it as it is. No offence meant."

* * *

The week went by. It was Friday afternoon. No need to go to the library today, Mark thought, as he gazed out of the staff room window. I've got a job now. The bell went and children spilled into the playground, heading towards the gates, revitalised by the thought of the weekend. He watched the pupils as they made their way out of school, calling to each other, saying goodbye, smiling, making arrangements, walking purposefully to where the buses lined up. There is an unspoken fellowship when school finishes on a Friday, he thought. We've got through the week. No doubt there will be unfinished business, issues to be resolved, hopes or fears for the weekend itself as well as the following week, but there is a sense of closing the chapter that has been the last five days. The goodbyes feel different to those shared on a Thursday.

It was going to take time to get used to things here but he felt it had been a good start. Much of his role seemed to be simply to be available, chatting with those who wanted (but he was still too new, and many were shy) or being asked to go into lessons to give a poem or a story. Colleagues in the staff room were friendly and he could understand the doubts of those such as Ed Moore.

Chapter 4: Links begin to be made

Monday morning saw him back in the Headmaster's study. "Did you have a good weekend?" Mr English asked.

"Yes, thank you, a trip to Dorset to see friends."

"Whereabouts?"

It struck Mark that this was the first occasion that the Headmaster had asked anything that was close to being a personal question.

"Shaftesbury," he answered. "Have you been there?"

"Yes."

The silence that followed was somehow unexpected to Mark. He felt he had to say something.

"Actually, I wrote a poem about it. This school must have worked some magic on me last week! As you know, I have not written much poetry before, and this one still seems hurried and unfinished to me, and…"

"Don't worry," interrupted Mr English. "Remember that we don't finish stories or poems. We offer where we have got to, where we have reached. It is the gift for the moment. But let's hear what you've done with Shaftesbury."

"Do you know Gold Hill? It sort of sweeps down…"

"I know Gold Hill," interrupted the Headmaster again. "Let's hear the poem."

Light spreading far across the land
Of hills and mists, of stones and thatch.
Speaking Alfred, Arthur, richness deep
Of gentle strength, of patient hope

And golden sun transforming all
To peace and sweeping eventide
Unchanging for a thousand years
As softening twilight gathers

Mr English looked up. "I would be interested to know why you included Arthur. I understand about Alfred and Wessex. But why Arthur?"

Mark was slightly surprised and perhaps a little put out. One or two of the later lines had pleased him and he would have liked them to be noticed. But he answered the question.

"I am not quite sure. Cadbury Castle, which some supposed to be the site of Camelot, is not very far away. And the view from the top of Gold Gill seems so old, as old as legends, if you know what I mean. And I like what I know of the Arthur stories." Mark hesitated and flushed slightly. "In fact..." And he paused again.

"I'm wondering if I am getting to know that look," smiled the Headmaster. "Have you written a poem about him as well?"

"Yes, I have," said Mark, recovering his good humour. "Here goes."

You may mock my fallen state, my pain and my betrayal
You may say I was naïve, that it's a sad and weary tale
You may break the blessed table and scorn the empty chairs
You may bring to wounded minds the pain of scandalous affairs

But there was good, I swear to that, and it was not in vain
Lamorak and Galahad, we hear the noble names
Merlin, Arthur, Guinevere, Lancelot and Kay
Shining light through stories, to brighten dreary days.

Nothing seemed to happen for a few moments and then Mr English stood up.

"Well, an interesting start to a Monday, we should chat more about it sometime. But perhaps not now, we must move on. Have you ever done any religious studies? Freda James has got her exam class; she says they are feeling rather jaded. Can you go in and help this morning?"

"Yes, she mentioned it on Friday."

"Excellent, your colleagues are already responding to you. They know you are here." Mr English smiled broadly. "Well done."

"I am not at all sure you have been revising as you should," Miss James was saying to her pupils as Mark walked in. "Next lesson I am going to give you a thorough test, exam questions and all. This morning, to keep our brains moving, Mr Lind, our new teacher, whom I am sure some of you will have met last week, will be giving us three poems to help us remember some of those key events we have studied."

Mark moved to the front of the class and began to read.

The wilderness widens,
Filled with silence.
No meaning.
Empty of friends or role, status or sense.
Just there

And he was in it for forty days,
That strange, significant number.
A length of time
to break or make a man.

When all is stripped away,
When only me is left.

He paused and looked around. Miss James gestured to him
to continue.

Making a living by helping the faithful, I thought I could work
* with some pride*
Keeping some order in this place of ritual, keeping it dignified
Providing, supplying, right coins a-plenty so their prayers
* could be heard for real*
My stall at the temple was familiar to many, I could always
* give a good deal*

And yes, I needed to cover my costs, I freely admit and will say
It may have been sad for those without cash, I'm sure they could
* find a way*
There was no need for anger or tables upturned, that all seemed
* excessive to me.*
There's enough going on in these difficult times without losing our
* dignity.*

He stopped again, and then pressed on:

The feast of freedom, death and hope.
Of love and fear entwined
When tired faces start awake,
As old words are revived

A little sip of wine, a broken crust of bread
That's all and that's enough
Saying, being, so much more
Than we can ever hold.

Miss James smiled. "Thank you, Mr Lind. Now everyone, I am sure that will help us remember what we should have learned this term. Robert, what were they about?"

"The temptations, the turning over tables in the temple, the Holy Grail," answered a tall dark-haired boy from the back.

"Good, good," said Miss James. "To be precise, the third one is about the Last Supper. The name Holy Grail is part of the stories that much later surround it, but that is not what the examiners will be looking for."

Another voice rang out. "Please Miss, how about Mr Lind doing a poem about the Holy Grail?"

"Gary, not now. Perhaps once I am sure you are on track for the exams, but now is not the time. Let's keep focused on the exams. Right everyone, exercise books out and let's get some more notes down. Who can remember the temptations in the desert?" Miss James smiled at Mark and he knew it was time to leave.

"How did the lesson go?" asked the Headmaster when they passed each other in the corridor later in the day.

"OK, I think. I did three poems and a child asked for a

fourth. However there wasn't really time and Freda moved us on."

"And wasn't there time?"

"Well, that's not really for me to say. I imagine she had her lesson planned and needed to keep things moving. Perhaps also she felt that if one child asked for a poem then they might all want one."

"I wonder how much of a problem that would really be," Mr English pondered. He smiled. "But perhaps if I were Freda I would have done the same. And, to be fair, I moved us on when we were talking this morning so you could get to her lesson in time. Let me muse for a while: can we have a storyteller and poet if we do not give time to hear them? That's something we need to consider.

"Anyway, we must move on (again!). There is a child, Emma Armstrong. I don't think she is very happy. She is doing things that are not in her best interests and something must be happening for her to reach this point. She used to like reading and has a good imagination, but now keeps that quiet (because at the moment she is keeping everything quiet). She is meeting you in your room at break tomorrow. I think it might help if you tell her a story."

"So we don't know what's wrong with her?" asked Mark

"I didn't say anything was wrong *with* her. But it is possible that something wrong has happened *to* her, or that she is involved *in* something wrong."

"I would be happy to help," said Mark, rather formally. "Sorry for using prepositions in a clumsy manner."

"Now you are irritated because I am so pedantic. Forgive me," Mr English said with a smile. "I rather like being careful with words. They matter so much, you see, they always carry weight. Prepositions especially."

Mark smiled. "I understand. I am still getting used to things. May I ask what sort of things she is doing that are damaging to herself?"

"You may ask but I think it best not to tell you."

As Mark stood to go, Mr English said, "Oh, one more thing, just out of interest: what was the subject of the extra poem the child in the lesson wanted?"

Mark told him.

Chapter 5: Making candles

The next day at the arranged time, Mark sat in his room opposite a girl whose hair successfully covered most of her face. "Emma, all I can say is that Mr English has asked me to tell you a story. I am probably as embarrassed as you are about sitting here and doing this, but here goes. Is that OK?"

The girl shrugged her shoulders.

Once upon a time there was an old candle-maker who lived in a village. People loved her candles: they were full of colours, beautifully shaped, and each one was different. One day a new candle-maker arrived. He opened his shop at the other end of the village. "There is room for two candle-makers," the villagers said, and all seemed well.

The new shop was a success. The candles were less expensive than the old ones. If cheaper means that you can get more candles, then that must be good. It was true that quite often the old candle-maker seemed to forget to charge at all, but her candles looked expensive and that made the careful villagers cautious. The new candles were also available immediately. You went into the shop and there they were. If you wanted a candle from the old shop, then you were often asked to come back later; or else the old candle-maker would keep you talking a long time and, well, not everyone had time for that these days. People got used to having different candles most days of the week from the new candle maker. None of them lasted long but the plentiful supply meant that this was not a problem.

The old shop began to look a little shabby. If you walked by you could still see the figure hunched over the table, presumably with her wax and her moulds and her knives, but it was hard to tell through the dusty window if much work was going on. But the village was glad she was there; the shop was a sign of stability and heritage, almost a curiosity.

Tom was a boy in the village and it was nearly his ninth birthday. His mother decided that something a little different was needed to mark the occasion. She found her way to the old candle shop (she suddenly realised that she had not been there for years) and ordered a special candle. She collected it three days later, managing to escape from the shop without being held up too long by the old woman's rambling conversation. When the candle was lit at Tom's birthday tea the colours seemed to fill the room. Golds and reds and greens shone and flickered, warm scents filled the room and it seemed to burn very, very slowly... By the end of tea it looked as if it had only just begun.

Tom wanted to know where this new candle was from. He called it the new candle because, although it was from the old shop, it was new to him. The next day his mother walked him to the other end of the village. Tom felt it all looked rather strange, much less smart than the other shops he was used to visiting. But he went in cheerfully enough, if a little nervously.

"You must be Tom," the old woman said. "Did you have a nice birthday?"

"Yes, thank you," said Tom, who was a polite child. He paused. "I liked the candle." He paused again. "I wondered how you made it so special."

The old woman gently started to scrape some dry wax off her wooden bench. She raised her head and looked again directly at Tom. "You liked the candle because it was made for you. Every time I make a candle I think about the

27

person who will receive it. I pour all those thoughts in with the wax and the colours and the scents." She stopped, as if wondering whether to carry on. But the boy was still attentive. "Tom, every candle I make is made with care and time, with care and time. There is no secret, no magic. It takes a little longer and seems inconvenient for those in a rush. I don't quite know how it works, but – well, it seems to work. It seems the best way."

Tom and his mother went home together. Only a few months afterwards the old candle-maker became ill and had to move many miles away to be closer to her niece. But Tom never forgot the memory of the old woman hunched over her work bench, nor the quiet old voice telling him how she made his candle.

Emma looked up. There was little expression in her face.

"May I go now, Sir?"

"Yes." said Mark "Thank you for coming along and for listening." She stood up, said nothing and left the room. Mark took a deep breath. Well, that didn't go very well, did it, he thought. You messed that up. You should have prepared better.

"Emma did not like your story," said Jenny when Mark bumped into her at the end of the day.

Oh great, thought Mark, the one thing worse than doing something wrong is being told you have done it wrong when you already know. And how does Jennifer Loss know, anyway? What's so special about her that Emma talks to her and won't say a word to me? And why can't she dress up the criticism in some sort of encouragement? I am still only new here, and…

Jenny interrupted his thoughts.

28

"I think that might be a good sign. I have asked her to come and tell you why not."

Mark was taken aback. "Do you know?"

"No. She simply told me that it had been a waste of time." She smiled and leaned forward. "But, Mark, I know that it would not have been, so something must have got to her that she reacted so strongly. And…You are not going to give up on a child just because she is a bit teenagerish, are you now?"

Mark felt his tension slide away.

"It's all good for my humility." And he smiled back.

The next morning Emma was in his room again. She remained standing. "I have only got two minutes because I need to see someone, but Miss Loss told me that I had to come and tell you that I did not like your story."

"Thank you for doing that, Emma," said Mark. He tried to keep his voice friendly but knew he was sounding stilted and tense. "Was it a bit sentimental? Or a bit magical, or…"

"No, I just didn't like it"

Mark took a deep breath. "I am sorry."

 Today she did not ask, she simply said: "I must go now."

And she did.

Mark sat silently for a few moments. He was just about to get up to go to the staff room to join his colleagues for the end of break when there was a knock on the door.

"Hello, come in," he called.

"Hello, Sir. Mr English told me to come to see you."

"Ah, you were in Miss James' class. It's Gary, isn't it?"

"Yes sir. Mr English asked me to ask you if you could stay after school and spend a few minutes with some of the students in Room 868." He said it in a slight rush, as if this was a sentence he had repeated many times in his head. He then continued: "And please could you be ready with your poem about the Holy Grail."

Chapter 6: Three gatherings

The staff room was usually full after lunch and Mark enjoyed sitting there while the conversation flew in all directions. He knew it would take more time to settle in completely but he was beginning to feel part of things.

Frank Edwards threw down the newspaper. "Another government initiative! Can't we persuade them all to go on sabbatical? Don't they understand that we need fewer, not more, of their crazy ideas? Mark, cheer us up, give us a poem."

Mark was no longer quite so taken aback by situations like this. Three minutes?" he asked.

"Three minutes. Hush everyone, Shakespeare is getting into gear!" called out a voice. The laughter was good-natured.

"I'm ready," said Mark after a few minutes.

It was decreed by someone at somewhere
That the carriage must move to the left
The neighbouring carriage was shunted
A little way down the track

It bumped and it pushed and it juddered
And another carriage was knocked.
This shuffled another one further
And a child, singing free, was squashed

The someone at somewhere claimed strongly
That they're under such pressure, too
The graphs and the headlines had led them to feel
That something just had to be done.

There was a mix of chuckles and mild applause.

"Well, I must transfer a bit of pressure to my lazy pupils," said Ed Moore. He yawned, got up and left the room. Mark went to sit next to Jenny.

"That was interesting," she said, when Mark sat down. "I wonder if we, too, can become experts in 'transferred pressure'. We can feel under pressure and then push and push those around us, building up pressure on them in all kinds of quiet ways. The sighs, the look, the unfair expectations, are all weapons that can be skilfully used. And unconsciously used, too, which perhaps is even more worrying. How many children are squashed because of the pressure that their parents or teachers face? How do we handle our own pressure, so we don't spoil things for others?"

Mark was not sure what to say.

Jenny continued, "You see, that's what you do, Mark, that's why it is important. You trigger trains of thought."

It was the end of the school day. As Mark walked along the corridor towards classroom 868 the autumn afternoon was fading outside. He opened the door and saw that the room was full. People were not sitting neatly in rows; they were perched everywhere, some on chairs, some on desks. There was a murmur of chatting. They were all facing the teacher's desk and on the middle of it was a candle. There was no other light.

He looked towards the desk. The faces nearer the candle were brighter. At first it was a little harder to see the faces further into the room but his eyes steadily grew accustomed to the light. As they did, things became clearer; he noticed Mr English towards the back, relaxed and chatting with a pupil. Jenny Loss was somewhere at the side. He gazed around. Issie and Jane were there. So, to his surprise, was Emma. Gary was sitting near the front.

"Thank you everyone," came the Headmaster's voice. "It is time to be quiet now. I think we are complete. Mr Lind, thank you very much for coming along. Do go and sit behind the desk. This is your session, not mine. I think you kindly have a poem for us?"

"Thank you, Headmaster," Mark replied and went to the desk. The candle was now between him and the faces. In the stillness the gathering silence strengthened. He began to speak.

Did the hands that shape the cup know the meaning it would hold?
Or see the deepening stories that unendingly unfold?
The wine, the blood, the vision, the quest across the sea
The strange and flowing riches that fashioned Glastonbury

Did the hands that share the cup know the searching it would bring
From knights and nameless pilgrims who wished to serve their king?
Did they sense the drawing power of all that lay within,
The fellowship, the sacrifice, of losing all to win?

The quiet of the room, the flicker of the candle flame, the faces young and old. We could be Saxons listening to a saga, thought Mark, relaxing after a feast in the thane's hall, with the wild dark outside.

The silence was held for a few moments. Then one or two of the younger pupils began to shuffle. The Headmaster's voice broke in, "Thank you Mr Lind. Now, Gary, why were you so keen for Mr Lind to read a poem about the Holy Grail?"

"I've been reading stories about it, Sir."

"Thank you Gary. Would you like to say more? Or does anybody else want to say something?" He paused and again there was silence. He held the pause longer. "No? Well, thank you all, it really is getting dark outside and some of you need to be getting home." He walked purposefully to the door, turned on the lights and stood there while everyone filed out.

Mark waited for the last to leave and then made his way to the door.

"Have you a few moments?" Mr English asked. "Just come along to my study for a chat, if you would be so kind."

When Mark arrived he was slightly surprised, but less than he would have been when he began at the school, to see that Gary was already there. He was considerably more surprised to see Emma. He joined them, Mr English and Jenny at the table.

There was a knock at the door.

"Sorry we're late," said Issie, breathlessly. She and Jane came in and found their spaces round the table.

"That all seemed rather brief," began Mark. "I am sorry if I should have prepared something longer; I…"

"The Grail is important – very important," the Headmaster interrupted. "It was right for all who wanted to hear the poem to have the opportunity to do so. But I did not want them to be taken further than they were ready to go or than they wished. Indeed I somewhat abruptly cut things short. All this is too important to be rushed. We travel *alongside* people, we do not drag them. Thus I did not press hard for further discussion or explanation. If anyone had commented we would have stayed and talked more. But there were no more comments and so it was right to stop. We must believe that the right words have power in themselves, we do not need layer on layer of superfluous sentences. We do not know the effect of what you said and we do not need to.

"Gary is here now because he prompted the poem, Emma because she was honest enough to say she did not like your story and I like honesty. Issie and Jane because, well, just because they are them, I like working in a team. Miss Loss because we need some common sense now and then. Robert, who first mentioned the Grail in the lesson in answer to your third poem, was not upstairs and I don't know his mind well enough to ask him here. But he chose not to join us to hear the poem, so perhaps he is not ready to be with us now."

"And the candle in the classroom?" asked Mark, thinking that he had never seen the Headmaster in this mood.

"A little self-indulgent of me. I suppose." said Mr English, and he smiled. "Perhaps it was a reminder of other times. Perhaps there is no harm in setting a scene, in creating an atmosphere. Somehow less artificial than those fluorescent strips, although I suppose the light in them is ultimately equally elemental."

"Why is it so important, Mr English? Not the light, the Grail. " asked Gary

"Because of what it has caused, and does cause, people to do," replied Mr English.

Mark was increasingly feeling out of his depth and felt the need to reach back to the shore. "Gary, you said 'is'. You should say 'was'. It doesn't exist now. Stories and poems are one thing; physical reality is another. It was a poem; I am sure Mr English would agree that this is not about some quest!"

"One thing you will learn about being at this school," said Mr English, "is that truth is absolute, even more important than customary unqualified affirmation of colleagues. Thus if you think I am wrong you must tell me, even in front of a pupil. If I think you are wrong, I similarly must say. It is all about respect and truth. Anyway, students think it fun when we disagree, don't they?"

The teenagers smirked slightly, nodded and looked expectant.

"Which was all an introduction to say that on this occasion I do not agree. The cup exists. If that meal happened, they would have had to drink out of *something*. Don't be distracted by the names or legends given to it over the centuries, we must keep our feet on the ground. What happened to that something they used, we do not know. Perhaps crushed to dust, hidden in some old monastery, buried in mud, in little pieces in some undiscovered first-century Jerusalem rubbish dump, perhaps on a trestle table in a jumble sale in a small town in Wales or Poland as we speak, or burned and the ashes dispersed across the world. Perhaps we are breathing atoms from it right now. But it exists. If something once existed it stays existing."

"In the stories I read," Gary said enthusiastically, "there was one that said it had been brought to Glastonbury, like you said in the poem, Mr Lind."

"People think that is extremely unlikely, but of course one never can be completely sure," answered Mr English. "The stories connecting Joseph of Arimathea to the Grail come much later, hundreds of years later. One can see why these stories grew, because the original story has it that Joseph was involved in burying the body but his link with the cup

36

is not mentioned by the early writers. And it is rather hard to know why his followers would have chosen Glastonbury, although I suppose that a convenient vision solves that problem. But the cup itself, used at that meal in Jerusalem all those years ago, somewhere, in dust or solid form, still exists. And just possibly it, or part of it, is in Glastonbury. But I repeat, that would be seen by most people as being very unlikely. It could be anywhere."

There was quiet.

"I agree I was wrong about the existence," said Mark. "But am I wrong about the quest?"

"The significance of the Grail is not what it was, or is, but what it was used for, what it pointed towards. You understood that in your poem. If someone like Gary is interested enough to ask for a poem about it then I want to ask whether that means there is a genuine search for the reality behind the stories. I want to know if there is an attraction, a calling, to the themes of sacrifice, forgiveness, new beginnings and heroism. I want to know if we have someone here who is willing to use strength well. The response to the calling could be called a quest, if you like to use such words."

Mark looked steadily at Mr English.

"Have you been involved in quests like this for a long time?"

The Headmaster replied calmly. "I have seen a few quests over the years."

It was Emma's turn to look up.

"If you don't mind me asking, Mr English, what is your first name?"

"Rex."

The Headmaster smiled at Emma, and Mark wondered what memories were stirring behind those friendly eyes. He glanced down at the table where they were sitting. A hundred questions swept through his mind. None of them, he thought, were the same as when he was 'interviewed' all those weeks ago.

"There, Mr Lind, I told you that Emma liked reading. Reading and being honest; and thus she made a leap, perhaps rather an important leap. But, everyone, I don't want us to be distracted by other issues. Gary, and perhaps others here sitting round this table, are interested in the Grail. You must stick with that for the moment and ask yourselves why. I am simply one of the cast, happening to be on stage as you say the key lines. I am holding the coats on the touchline, it is you who are playing the game." The Headmaster paused and looked at his watch. "Now you younger ones, it really is time to be on your way home. It is a little later than usual. Go carefully and safely, as always."

Chapter 7: Preparing for battle?

It had been an unsettling end to a Monday, reflected Mark. It was partly because of the unusual reference points that Mr English used; there seemed to be so many layers in him, and what bubbled to the surface seemed to come from depths that were beyond Mark's comprehension. It was partly because of Jenny's comment about triggering trains of thought – if she knew how inadequate he felt, she wouldn't believe that. What will happen if I say something very stupid? What trains of thought will be started then? He felt he was a fraud, and that it was only a matter of time before he was found out.

But the next day was a new day and, like all mornings in a school, there was no slow start. As soon as he arrived there were people to see, notices to hear, choices about time to be made. Unlike his colleagues, he was not tied to the classroom, but his days felt very full. He had learned not to be surprised by who might be knocking on his door. But quarter past eight was early for the first visitor.

"Come in, come in," he called.

There stood Emma. "Hello, Sir. I wanted to say sorry that I had to go quickly yesterday morning."

He motioned to her to sit down, and she did.

"Thank you, Emma, for saying that. That means a lot. Is it a better time now for me to ask why you didn't like the story?"

"I'd rather not say."

But then she continued, "I liked the poem about the Grail and I read more about it last night. Do you think people once really thought it was powerful and could change things? Do you think it still exists somewhere?"

"I have never thought about it very much; and if you have been looking things up then you now probably know more than I do. But, as Mr English said, if it ever existed it could be anywhere, in smithereens or on someone's mantelpiece. But, tell me, Emma, what is it that you would change if you found it? What do you want the power for?"

"I'd rather not say any more." Her eyes were not quite cold again, but the barriers were going up.

"Shall we leave it there?" asked Mark, realising he had moved too quickly.

"Yes." But she did smile slightly as she made for the door. "Thank you."

***

Mr English was speaking to the school in assembly.

"What are the seven foes? The modern world forgets. Perhaps because of a strange mix of ignorance and arrogance we forget that the wisdom of the ancients was gathered and built in a world where daily life was usually a struggle. A world with no anaesthetics and few comforts. If you want wisdom that will stand the test of time, go to those who lived when life was hard.

"Ira, Acedia, Superbia, Luxuria, Avaritia, Gula, Invidia. Pretty-sounding names, but names that promise both attraction and destruction. Wrath, Sloth, Pride, Lust, Greed, Gluttony, and Envy. The seven deadly sins, the cardinal sins, the capital vices, call them what you will.

40

They walk the earth. They devour like dragons; one of them may be eating you up even as I speak. My task this morning is a simple one. I am to explain them, and remind you of their adversaries, our friends, the seven virtues. What you do with that knowledge is in your hands.

"Ira is wrath. Good anger can be a positive impulse to get things done, it can be our way of pushing hard for justice. But this sort of anger, this *Ira*, is when we lose control, or when our arguments or cause are weak and we dishonestly seek for inappropriate weapons. This anger is about selfish frustration, not the righteous seeking of justice. It is surprisingly habit-forming.

"The counter virtue is *patientia*, patience. Understanding the strength that lies in waiting, trusting that other forces are at work and it is not for us to decide the fate of the world using only our passion as a guide. Learning from nature and experience that to build tall you have to dig deep.

"Acedia is sloth. Deliberately deciding we cannot be bothered, hoping someone else will do it, not interested in developing our talents and character. Not realising that time itself is a gift.

"In opposition to *Acedia* is *Industria*, diligence. The taking of responsibility, the doing of the task even when we do not want to do it. It is not about becoming a workaholic; a diligent person will ensure that there is rest and play as well as work. It is about wanting, for the sake of others, to make the most of who we are and what we can do.

"Superbia, pride, destroys relationship and community. It is believing we need no one else. It is saying that my needs and my views are the most important and that no other person is quite as important as me. A person eaten up by

41

pride cannot truly live in relationship with others. It is sometimes seen as the deadliest foe of all.

"*Humilitas*, humility, is the obvious counter. Seeing ourselves as we truly are. Recognising and affirming the gifts of others and enjoying being part of the team. Not rushing for the limelight. Knowing that we need each other.

"*Luxuria* is lust, deciding that sexual desire is to dominate my thinking about the other person. No longer really seeing them as a person at all, simply as a means of gratification for me.

"And so to chastity, *Castitas*, recognising the whole value of the person, determined not to cloud or destroy the respect and relationship by allowing sexual desire to dominate. Being prepared to fight to gain the necessary self-discipline.

"*Avaritia*, greed, cannot be satisfied. It is when we want more for me, for me, for me. It may be greed for money, status, popularity or anything else. We set up meaningless goals, are greedy for them, and invest all our efforts and energy to try and stretch closer to them. But these goals do not deliver what they promise.

"And so the opposite needs to be *Caritas*, charity. A looking outwards to the needs of others, a generosity of heart that means our interests are not always put first. Knowing that giving is part of our calling. True charity will involve some sacrifice but it will set free. Greed only enslaves.

"*Gula* is Gluttony. Losing control. Not only wanting more of something (especially food, but not only that), but wanting it now, impatiently, selfishly, uncontrollably. It is interesting that the ancients believed that gluttony as well as greed should be in this list. Perhaps these are more dangerous temptations than we think.

"Its opposite is *Temperantia*, temperance, developing the necessary self-control. Recognising that it is a sign of strength to know when we have had enough. Having the courage, strength and self-awareness to be moderate. Having the discernment to know the difference between what will lead us astray and what will see us safely home.

"And finally *Invidia*, envy. Never being satisfied with one's own gifts and blessings. Angry or unhappy that others may apparently have more praise or money or status. It nearly always involves a misreading of the situation. It is profoundly destructive to relationships, always seeing them in terms of competition, not in terms of complementary strengths.

"Developing *Humanitas,* kindness, is the counter to envy. Doing good and helpful acts to others. Celebrating when they are doing well. Enjoying the act of giving. Asking how we can build up, not pull down. If every word in every school or home was marbled through with *Humanitas* we would be able to live very different lives.

"We notice that these foes have two things in common. At root they are all selfish. And they can become all-consuming and habit-forming. They are addictive and they grow. Lust leads to deeper lusts. Angry moments lead to anger habits. Envy of one becomes envy of many.

"Be watchful against them, and remember the seven virtues, the seven friends. Have we got patience, diligence, humility, chastity, charity, temperance, kindness? None of us have them as much as we would like, but, at the very least, do we want them? The wanting of them, of any of them, is a very powerful weapon."

"What was all that about?" Mark asked Jenny after assembly. "Why was that on his mind? Why did he do that today?"

"I don't know," she replied. "But he has a habit of doing things like that. He may have decided that there is someone who particularly needed to hear one of those sentences, but that it was better to be general than specific. He can be like a cook, mixing a particular ingredient into a wider meal because he knows that one of those who sit at his table will not eat that ingredient if it is served on its own. It can be rather unsettling when he gets carried away like that but it is likely that there was a specific purpose behind it. And even if not, he is a man who believes some things simply need to be said, must be said, however they are received."

"He is difficult to read, isn't he?" said Mark. "You know him very well. There seems to be so much under the surface with him."

"It seems like that because that is how it is," said Jenny, slightly briskly. "Now, any chance of coming into a lesson and doing some Shakespeare riddles? Only three or four. I need to wake up my sixth form a little."

"I'd be pleased to" he said, not quite sure if the change of subject was deliberate or not. He followed her to her room and after the usual introduction, he began.

Fooled by words of fleeting fame
A king in name but not in truth.
Hastening time, too much, too soon.
Hurrying to win but losing all
Worn through by evil and despair
Fading, stumbling, crashing. To his end.

The small group looked hesitant.

Jenny said, "If I have guessed this right, Mr Lind might have included something about betrayal of friends, or betrayal of a king. Or witches."

"Macbeth!" someone called out.

Mark nodded. "Here's another one."

In forest paths we're found and lost
And lives are turned and veils grow thin
And worlds collide and plays entwine
In mixed and magic, dangerous dark.

Jenny looked across at Mark and then looked at her pupils. "A Midsummer Night's Dream?" she asked, rather thoughtfully, without waiting for a response from the class. "That was an interesting part of a comedy to choose. Thank you, Mr Lind, we had better be getting on with our lesson now."

Mark left, wondering why his visit to the class had been shorter than he expected.

Chapter 8: A Christmas story

The weeks passed by. The school was getting ready for Christmas. One lunchtime, Issie and Jane appeared in the doorway of Mark's room.

"Your room needs decorating," announced Issie. "Look, we've brought some left-over tinsel and things from our classroom." Jane shrugged and smiled behind her friend. They clambered about the room, draping decorations from pictures and shelves.

"Thank you so much," said Mark, slightly taken aback and sitting in the centre of a sudden whirl of activity. "This is very kind."

"Issie's idea," Jane said. "She is always so impulsive. I really hope you don't mind us barging in like this."

"Do you ever do a Christmas poem or a story?" asked Issie. "I know, how about that knight you told Mr English about in your interview? Get him to do something for Christmas."

Mark replaced an end of tinsel that had already fallen from the edge of a shelf and sat down. The girls sat down opposite him. He smiled. "Thank you for remembering." He paused for a few moments and then began.

Sir Richard waited by the great doors leading out of the castle.

"Is this wise?" asked Catherine.

"It is worth trying."

"I can always rely on you not to give a straight answer if you don't want to," Catherine said with a smile. "Wise or not, I know you feel you have to do this."

He smiled at her and then nodded to two guards who swung open the doors. Sir Richard rode out over the drawbridge and trotted across a field. The horse left clear tracks in the winter snow. After an hour he arrived at a hamlet. He stopped at a church, tied up his horse, paused for a moment as he looked around, and went in.

It was cold.

A figure was sitting on the front pew on the left of the church. It did not turn to look but, on hearing the footsteps, simply said, "I got your message." The voice was not calling out, or raised.

Sir Richard walked down the aisle and sat on the pew on the right. The two men, both thick-set and strong, both heavily clothed against the cold, gazed ahead.

"Thank you for agreeing to meet," Sir Richard began.

"Are we discussing a truce? Will you be realistic? Are you prepared to let me hold what I have gained?"

"No," replied Sir Richard. "And I am not here to talk about that at all. I want to widen your perspective, we are here to look." He gestured upwards, and in the left of the east window a picture of the Bethlehem stable was marked out in the stained glass. He then pointed right to a figure in an adjoining window. He was stately and richly dressed, two soldiers stood obediently by him, but his face was troubled.

"Herod," said Sir Richard. "A man of power and status. Of greed and thus of fear."

47

"Spare me your lessons. My time is precious. And your time may be shorter than you think."

"It is not your time or my time. We do not own time. We are in it, and in it we decide to do what is best." Sir Richard's voice became harder. "You forget who I am and what I can do. I saw your men in the shadows behind the pillars. I saw the footprints in the snow leading to the side door of the church. But I am a Miril and you touch me at your peril. You would be wise to listen to me.

"Look at those two windows, Adam. Which of those images is remembered and celebrated now? Think about where honour truly rests, what power really is and how it should be used. How do you want to be remembered?"

The other man looked across at him. "What is a Miril but a name? The supposed glory of the past means nothing. I am in the present and I deserve a good share of this land. A faded title will not stop me."

"Look at those two windows," repeated Richard. "How do you want to be remembered?" He stood up. A slight movement from the other man caught his eye. He turned round and faced two soldiers walking towards him, their hands nearing the hilts of their swords. He saw a slight hesitation in their eyes and he walked straight at them, his own sword still in his scabbard. They hesitated and, grim-faced, he walked through them as they parted before him. But they did not raise their swords against him.

As he rode slowly back to the castle he glanced across the fields through the gathering dusk, picking out the soft lights beginning to glow in the cottage windows. He knew the names of those who lived there, knew who would be gathered round each hearth. He knew who would be feeling strong this Christmas, and who would not. They

48

were his people. The trees around were still and silent, dark against the snow.

Mark stopped.

The girls sat quietly. "I feel it is like one of Mr English's candle moments," said Jane.

The bell went.

"It's time for lessons," sighed Issie. "We'd better go."

"Thank you for the decorations," said Mark.

"Thank you for not minding us turning up, but it was rather fun," said Jane, and the girls went out. Just outside the door Issie turned and said quietly, "May I talk to you sometime?"

"Of course, of course," Mark assured her, "Any time."

Chapter 9: The challenge

Ed Moore held the note in his hand.

"You were right to tell me what he did in assembly. It would seem that the gloves are off. It sounds like a deliberate and direct challenge to you and indeed to us (I assume you were not taken in). Or he may be looking to strengthen his position and build up his little group. Whatever it was, it is important he does not cause more harm. It is time to act."

Ed read it again and put it in his pocket.

***

"Mr Moore has a notice for us this morning," said Mr English in assembly later in the week.

Ed Moore's notice was about ambition. He told the students that they were talented people and that the school would always work hard to help them be the best they could be. He hoped they would achieve the recognition due to them. In order to help them think about this he had invited a speaker to visit the school at lunchtime. Everyone was welcome.

The event was not compulsory, but Mr Moore was a popular teacher. It was raining outside and there was not much else going on. About fifty pupils were there in the hall. Mark went along. He thought his presence would be seen as being supportive. Ed had been pleased when he had heard he would be there.

"It gives me great pleasure to introduce Ms F. L. Morgan." Ed, dressed in a smart cream suit, was finishing his opening words. "Her insights have helped thousands of students in many schools. Ms Morgan, over to you." He began a brief round of applause.

"You can be the best." she began in a compelling voice. "Dream your dreams, it is your dreams that matter. It is you who should be the star. Go for it, be bold for it, deserve it, strive for it. Anything is possible. There is nothing that you cannot do if you dream the dream. Don't disappoint the expectations that others have of you. Don't let them down."

Mark shifted in his seat.

"There will be a time when you can watch out for others but your first priority is to watch out for yourself. It is you that wants to achieve the best. It is you that wants to be first. We need people like you to reach for the stars."

Mark grew more uncomfortable.

"And don't be too coy as to how get there. It is a tough world out there. We are talking about destinations, not journeys; ends, not means."

Mark did not know what to do. I am here to be supportive to Ed, he thought. There is an issue of professional loyalty. I am not going to stand up, make a fool of myself, and antagonise him.

But reluctantly, heavily, Mark rose to his feet.

Fifty pairs of eyes swivelled towards him. The speaker stopped. Ed Moore looked at him sharply from the stage.

"Mr Lind, there will be an opportunity for questions at the end. It is our usual practice at *this* school to allow the speaker to finish."

51

Mark looked around. He saw the faces of students and colleagues whom he was beginning to feel he was getting to know. He saw a mixture of confusion and embarrassment. He liked it here. Why was he spoiling everything?

"Er, of course, I just wanted to say that I am happy to do a poem at the end if you and Ms Morgan wish."

That was not what he had stood up to say.

Ed Moore spoke coldly. "Thank you very much, Mr Lind, but it is not that sort of event. I think we will be able to manage without one of your little rhymes."

Ms Morgan finished about ten minutes later. There were one or two questions from the floor and then a pupil asked:

"Please, Sir, may we have Mr Lind's poem now?"

Ed Moore looked across at Ms Morgan, who held up her hands in a gesture of resignation and smilingly said, "of course".

Mark slowly stood up again.

"No, I think it would be better if I…"

"Come now, Mr Lind," said Ed. "You have raised expectations. Of course we must hear it."

Mark looked around, trying not to let his nervousness show too much, and began to speak.

They'll never want to take your picture
They'll never ask your views
They'll never name you in the lists
You'll never hit the news

But you give time in quiet care for someone who's in need
Whose burdens you will lighten with faithful words and deeds.
You feed the poor and give them hope and walk the extra mile
You welcome and encourage, and give another smile.

There's another gallery, where pictures never fade
There's another honours list, where names are ever saved
If earthly glory passes you then worry not at all
We're playing on a bigger stage, and in a richer hall.

Mark sat down. All was quiet. And then one person began to clap, and then another. And then more joined in. The applause grew stronger and louder, as if a ripple was turning to a stream, then to a waterfall. Ed, who had sat down while the poem was being read, stood up. The applause faded. Silence fell.

***

Later in the staff room, Ed Moore, hand gripped round his mug of coffee so tightly that his knuckles were white, tackled him.

"Was that deliberate?"

"Not really, it is what came to mind."

"Well, you should have left it in what you call your mind. You deliberately, publicly, spoiled my meeting. I feel undermined. You also appear to have wanted to go out of your way to disagree publicly with an invited guest. We

53

don't treat each other like this at this school. I am not impressed, Mr Lind, not impressed at all."

Mark made his way towards the door. He hated any sort of scene. But Ed was standing close to the doorway. Mark was never quite sure how events then unfolded. He was leaving hurriedly and whether he bumped into Ed's elbow or Ed stepped forward into his path he could not tell. Whatever the cause, the arm was jolted and the coffee splashed from the cup.

All over Ed's suit.

His face was thunderous. Whether or not he had stepped forward a minute earlier, he certainly was doing so now.

Mark panicked and rushed through the door.

***

"I understand that you intervened in Ms Morgan's talk and there was then an altercation in the staff room?" asked Mr English, quietly.

The two of them were sitting in the Headmaster's study.

"I was not sure it was a helpful way of addressing a topic," began Mark. "It may be fine for those who have good dreams and who need encouragement. But what do we do for those children who cannot fulfil their dreams? How do we prepare them for the reality of being, in this language, second best? How do they know if their dreams are the right ones? They may think they win, but what if they are running the wrong race?"

"The questions you raise are valid. It may or may not have been a mistake to interrupt, but there was also the incident in the staff room?"

Mark went very quiet. This was his first full-time job for a year. He always found it difficult to shake off mistakes and failures and something in Mr English's voice made him wonder if this would not easily be set aside. He calmed his voice.

"I am sorry. I will go and find Ed and apologise. I will do my best to sort it out."

"He may not want it sorted out."

Feeling out of his depth, Mark left the room. He was very cross with himself but also slightly cross that he did not feel he knew what was going on.

Chapter 10: Ave atque Vale

However nothing was said the next day and the week finished quietly. The following Monday a message reached Mark that he was invited to Room 868 at the end of the day.

On the desk was the lighted candle. Circles of faces around it, each lit to a different level by the flame. Mr English's voice came out of the shadows.

"Mr Lind, do you remember your poem about Arthur? Please say it again."

Mark searched his mind for the moment. He recalled the words and began to speak.

You may mock my fallen state, my pain and my betrayal
You may say I was naïve, that it's a sad and weary tale
You may break the blessed table and scorn the empty chairs
You may bring to wounded minds the pain of scandalous affairs

But there was good, I swear to that, and it was not in vain
Lamorak and Galahad, we hear the noble names
Merlin, Arthur, Guinevere, Lancelot and Kay
Shining light through stories, to brighten dreary days

The Headmaster had been sitting near the back. He walked forward and found a space in the circle closest to the candle. A couple of the pupils shuffled apart and he sat between them.

"Was the table a blessed one?" he asked, thoughtfully. "I was grateful you used that word. It implies that some good may yet have been done."

He paused and looked around. "Forgive me, everyone, if I speak for a while. But you will have already guessed by my invitation to this room this afternoon that I may have something to say.

"An individual can do very little by themselves, which is one of the deep truths so often forgotten. And so, it was never *my* round table, it was *ours.* It was not easy. People will sometimes want to be part of it without knowing what the cost will be. Some think it is only about using their strength to help the weak and that indeed is very important. But equally important is the giving up of using the strength to glorify oneself. Not once in a moment of passion and conviction, but every day, every single day. Laying aside the thirst for personal status and advancement. Moment by moment, day by day. It is about sacrifice. This is a round table, here is equality, there is no first seat to be grasped.

"If you gather the best and the brightest to be your knights then each one would, in the eyes of others and perhaps of themselves, have been destined for fame and success. You ask them to lay that down. No, it is not easy. And so there were tensions and unconscious competitiveness among these striving, perfectionist knights. Rescuing the needy from giants or monsters (which come in all sorts of shapes) became more about the magnificent way we killed the enemy rather than the needs of the rescued. The search for the Holy Grail became more about the search than the Grail. And, equally mistakenly, it had already become more about the Grail than what the Grail points to. It is a common temptation: people remembered the way I found Excalibur, but they forget what I used it for.

"But people were willing to *try*. And there was something about it that sometimes felt blessed and I am grateful to be reminded. Much good was achieved, many were rescued, strong friendships were forged. We encouraged each other to do what is right. We feasted and laughed and perhaps the story has helped people down the years. Perhaps it did make a difference to their lives, a book or film cheering a rainy afternoon, good values permeating attitudes and actions.

"Part of the story, as some of you know, was the betrayal. Allow me to say a poem myself, given to me by one of Mr Lind's predecessors in another place, another time.

The dreamy days, the lazy walks, the silent pacts to stay
The gentle light, the shining eyes, the words no need to say.

She and I used to say those lines to each other. But I was often, understandably, put in the shade by the more dynamic comrades. I lost her to a friend. Lancelot was a soaring star and I could understand the attraction. Was it inevitable? Very little is, so I doubt it, but sometimes it felt like it was. I said very little but such wounds were not easily healed. It is confusing when a friend betrays you. But, you need not now be concerned, she knows how much it hurt and the healing has been given and received. I want you to remember that. There can always be forgiveness. She knows I am saying this to you this afternoon. We both want you to be people of hope.

"But was I then weaker when the next threat came? I think I was, weaker and slower. And increasingly reluctant to use my strength. Rather like the first story you gave us at your interview, Mr Lind. And emotionally of course I was bound up in Mordred. I did not want to destroy him.

"Those of you who know the story may remember that it is told that Arthur sleeps, ready to return in the hour of England's greatest need. It is not quite like that, I am called to all kinds of situations. Usually only for a short time. I do not fully know what my task is to be, I am

58

simply *there*. I was called to this school. And now I am called to leave.

"And once again, the table will be taken away and the chairs will be empty, put aside to be brought back another day. But what has happened remains forever. If something exists, it cannot cease to exist. We sow the seeds, do what we should, are watchful for the needy and search for truth. It was not all in vain. What is good, never is."

Mr English stopped speaking.

There was quiet and people slowly began to leave the room. Seven remained. Mr English, Emma, Issie, Gary, Jane, Jenny and Mark. They moved closer and they were now the circle around the candle.

The silence remained, but it was not uncomfortable or awkward. After a time, Jenny said, "I think it time for us to go." And she led the way to the door. Jane, Gary, Emma and Issie walked down the corridors to make their way home. Mr English stayed in the room. Jenny and Mark went to the staff room.

***

"I don't understand this at all." Mark said, when they got there.

Jenny looked at him thoughtfully. "So you don't know?"

"No," Mark replied.

"Rex has decided to leave the school. Ed has powerful connections on the board; a few phone calls last week and pressure began to mount. Rex undoubtedly could have stayed and fought it out. After all, he could hardly be blamed for a speaker being interrupted and a cup of coffee being spilled. It was not an important moment anyway, but he simply decided that this chapter was over."

"I still don't understand," said Mark, sounding rather desperate. "How could one mistake on my part cause this to happen? How did I get things so wrong?"

"Just because the consequences were not what you wished does not necessarily mean your decision was wrong. I was there, Mark, I was watching. I think she knew you were getting uncomfortable and so she kept pushing, kept saying outrageous things, becoming a caricature of herself, until you would react. I think Ed was playing his part, too. He saw an opportunity to have that poem read while pretending he did not want you to read it. He guessed what would be in it (you can take that as a compliment). All rather clever. And then he did enough to cause a scene in the staff room."

"How about the person – I still don't know who it was – who funded my position?"

"It was Ed. Quite a clever move. I think what happened was this: when he heard of the idea for a storyteller, Ed wondered if Rex was overreaching himself. Sooner or later a figure such as this might say the wrong story, give the wrong poem, intervene at the wrong moment. Storytellers are risky people to have around. This would make the Headmaster look as if he had made a big mistake in the appointment. So Ed supported the idea and even offered to fund it. He is quite rich. Last week he withdrew the funding, put on some pressure and threatened to publicise the news that the Headmaster had got it all wrong."

"So it was all set up," said Mark, flatly.

"It may have been, but Rex is bigger than that, much bigger. He wanted you because he knew that it was right for you to be here. Perhaps he had in mind one particular pupil who needed to hear what you said during Ms Morgan's lecture. Or even a comment or a smile that you gave in the corridor as you walked past someone. We may never know who that pupil was but Rex plays a deep and a long game. Always has. For Rex, losing, or rather changing, his job would count for nothing compared to knowing the right words were said at the right time."

***

The next morning Mark watched from the staff room window as the van was loaded up. He saw boxes of books being carried to it and four men struggling to lift Mr English's round desk down the main school steps and up the ramp. It was heavier than they expected. He turned away and realised that Ed Moore was standing next to him.

"A shame of course, such a shame," said Ed. "But chapters come to an end and new ones begin. I am sure Mr English will find a place elsewhere, somewhere appropriate for his undoubted talents. I don't know if you have heard the news but I am sorry of course that it might be difficult for you to stay with us in these times of financial constraint. Well, you know how these things are."

"I had not realised that you would be responsible for such a decision," answered Mark, realising he was sounding rude.

"Ah, you may not have heard what the real, serious, academic, teachers have been told by now," said Ed, and the contempt was no longer hidden. "I have been appointed acting Headmaster, so perhaps I am responsible for such a decision after all." He turned away.

Mark spoke slightly louder than usual: "Just one more thing, before we finish the conversation. May I give you a poem? I thought I would remind you about St George, as our school is named after him. Or had you forgotten?"

It was clear from Ed Moore's expression that he had no desire to hear any poems or stories, but there were other colleagues dotted round the staff room and courtesies must be observed. He turned back to face Mark and raised his hands in a resigned fashion.

Mark began:

The dragons never mean to harm, at least that's what they claim
And they appear at many times, wearing subtle names
Destroying and devouring, manipulating dreams
Smilingly explaining that the strongest have to feed

But Georges of this world use power differently
Their strength is bound by solemn vows to laws of chivalry
Any fool can hurt the weak or mockingly crush down
But real knights will rescue, and restore the rightful crown.

Ed Moore spoke coldly. "Thank you, Mr Lind, I wish you well for the future."

Mark turned and walked to the door. When he reached it he paused and looked back.

"You don't wish me well for the future at all, because you know that if I have a good future then that will be bad news for you. We are on different sides. Watch yourself, Ed, you are the sort of person who wins the little victories while not understanding the real battle. Sometimes in winning we lose. That's what has happened to you here. One day you may understand that."

"You are a fool, Lind. You patronise me and pretend to feel sorry for me, but I am the one still in a job and with more power here than you ever realised. You have got nothing. Go back to the list of vacancies. Go back to being on the margins. You have played with the big boys here and you have lost."

Ed Moore and Mark Lind stood and looked at each other. As if frozen in time.

Ed shook his head and walked out, straight past Mark without a glance.

Where did that all come from? Mark wondered. I'm not usually like that at all.

Chapter 11: Loose ends left untied

Mark Lind had lost his job. But the library was still the library. Books lovingly or urgently written, books prompted by demands of publishers, inner inspiration, readers or accountants. Books of stories and poems and information. Briefly, thought Mark, making his way to the broad tables on the first floor, I was part of what those writers were trying to do. Not very successfully though. A few hurried poems and stories, none of them very good, none of them having much effect. It was the first Friday in January. He picked up the newspaper from the rack, carried it to the table and opened it at the vacancies. There was nothing that looked likely, there was no need to reach for his notebook. Next week I must call the supply agencies and the schools. Next week I am available again. He got up and decided to go home.

In the hallway there was an envelope marked with his name. He picked it up, went up to his flat, sat on the edge of the bed and opened it. Inside was a poem.

My mum and dad are beautiful and that's because they're mine.
Others think they're rather odd, others think them strange
The things they say, the clothes they wear, they have their little ways
But I think they are beautiful, and that's because they're mine

They don't treat each other so, I find this hard to grasp
The damning words come flooding out and they don't seem to see
That when they hurt each other they're also hurting me

Underneath was written:

Dear Mr Lind,

I hope you don't mind me writing. Mr English gave me your address. Thank you for not pressing about why I did not like the candle-maker story. Adults always want to know the private things and I was not ready for that.

But you might be able to guess. Something about my dad preferring cheap candles.

Don't worry about replying. Thank you for all you did at school.

Yours sincerely

Emma Armstrong.

PS. I hope it was ok that I wrote a poem. I didn't mean to copy being you. It just felt right to write something.

Mark stayed sitting on the edge of his bed. Should he try to track Emma down and renew contact? He also remembered that Issie had not come back for the chat she had mentioned. Should he have done more? Had something happened? He would never know. He had been a very small piece of the jigsaw. The story is always unfinished. Someone else would be there for them if they wanted to talk again. It was time for him to move on. But he wished he had done more.

The weeks went by. He began to question how accurately he had remembered what had happened. Some moments had seemed almost magical, but now and again he wondered if it had simply been atmosphere. Autumn days and candles, stories and poems. Nothing more than that. It was just a phase. An impressive but impulsive Headmaster. It was time for him to move on.

Chapter 12: Nine years later

Watching the dawn is about seeing the world more clearly. Shadows separating and taking shape. Darkness lightening to shades of grey. And then the colours come. It is only later, if at all, that we see the sun that gives the light that brings the colours to life.

Emma had slept fitfully and by five in the morning she was in the old armchair, her mind gently turning as she looked out at the early morning light.

Dawn brings shapes, then clarity, then colour. If I had turned on the light at the wrong time, I would not have seen the dawn as it is. The artificial would have blinded me to the real.

Watching the dawn is about seeing things more clearly. But what if you don't want to? What if the blur is enough?

The thoughts began to fade. She could indeed begin to see glimmers of the morning. Perhaps it would not be cloudy and overcast after all.

Enough of this. She shook herself and got up from the chair.

It was seven years since Emma had left St. George's. A college course and now a job in a shop.

***

Mark rested his head against the train window, knowing it would not be long before the vibrations became uncomfortable. For the moment there was a reassuring rhythm and the glass was cool. He was tired, and if he leant the other way his head would be resting on the shoulder of a formidable-looking lady. That, he felt, would be inappropriate.

He had agreed to come to this reunion. The idea of them getting together had some appeal and it would remind him of interesting times. That brief chapter in his story which refused to be ignored. What had happened in those few months had happened; nothing that exists stops existing. He smiled at the memory and the voice behind it.

The window became uncomfortable. He sat upright and tried to concentrate on his book.

Gary was driving fast and confidently. It had been a good day. The interview had gone well and, even better, quickly; he had been able to write and file the article by noon and then begin making contacts as he chased a story to follow up on Monday. His editor seemed happy. He lived a busy life. New possibilities were emerging, he had got used to living quickly and sharply, seizing the moment. And now he was looking forward to the weekend. Like most journalists, he enjoyed the buzz and the challenge of being with people in any context, and who knows what may come of renewing a few old links?

Why isn't there more legroom on this coach? Jane shifted her position again. She was feeling annoyed with herself; she could have easily afforded the train and one change would not have been too troublesome. But the coach had been cheaper, if slower. She relaxed and smiled wryly at her decision. So typical.

***

By late afternoon Emma was waiting, standing in the sitting room. The holiday cottage was cared for and well equipped. There was a garden backing on to some woods.

Supper would be cooked and sent over from the neighbouring farmhouse. She went into the kitchen and filled the kettle. There was time for a cup of tea before they arrived.

As Mark walked out of the station he saw a familiar face.

"Jane?"

"Mr Lind?"

There was a pause. Then Jane said: "Did you come by train? I've just got off the coach. I'm glad you are here. How do we get to the house? Shall we walk?"

"Let's share a taxi," said Mark.

The taxi and Gary arrived at the cottage within ten minutes of each other. Emma welcomed them.

Half an hour later, rooms visited and bags unpacked, they gathered in the small dining room. Food arrived from next door and conversation began to flow. Nothing serious, simply some gentle updating as to what they were all doing, and had been doing, since they left St. George's. As the plates were being collected there was a natural pause.

Gary leaned forward:

"Right, now, Emma. Is this it? You have got us here – what have you got in store for us?"

"I don't know. I had a letter. As simple as that. It was to invite you here for the weekend. I don't know why. But it was signed R.E. and so I wondered."

Jane looked up and said calmly and warmly, "Who else could it be?"

68

Gary shifted in his chair and his smile hardened and then began to fade. "It could be. I don't know. Well, of course it probably is. But all that was a long time ago. We were, some of us were, well, children then. I think I have moved on. It was teenage stuff. Rather strange and unclear and best left behind.

"I hope you don't mind me saying this," he continued, "But it feels odd being only the four of us, and one of us being a teacher. I misunderstood the invitation. I thought there might be quite a group here, a real reunion. This all feels a little intense. No offence, Mr Lind."

"Don't worry." said Mark, "I agree, I feel rather out of place as well. Presumably Mr English will turn up at some point? Did he say anything about that?"

"No," said Emma. "All the letter said was to send the invitations. The cottage was booked for us. I don't know anything more than you."

"Do you know why the letter came to you, and not to any of the rest of us? And this does seem quite an inconvenient place," asked Gary.

"I don't know." Emma's voice was quavering a little now. "I feel like I'm being interrogated. The letter came. I did the best I could. I did what I thought I should do."

"Nine years ago all this sort of stuff led to the loss of a fairly decent Headmaster and the school going downhill from then. That didn't feel all that great," said Gary.

"But it was his idea then and it sounds like it's his idea now," said Jane.

"Exactly," said Gary. "You can understand my reluctance to sing for joy. Or of course someone could be playing games with us all. Is Issie coming?"

"I am not sure, there was no reply," said Emma.

There was a pause.

"Gary," said Jane, "I think Emma did what any of us would have done. Let's not give each other a hard time."

Gary shrugged and looked away from the others, drumming his fingers on the arm of his chair.

Chapter 13: Making music well

"Have you kept in touch since you left St. George's?" Mark asked. "Were you still friends in your last two years, after I left?"

"Sort of," replied Emma. "It felt a bit different. Jane and I and Gary used to meet up now and then at school. Issie seemed to withdraw a little and we lost touch, or at least I did."

"So did I," Gary added flatly.

Jane looked thoughtful. "Well, since we four are here, and we don't know why, I think we should ask Mr Lind for a story."

Mark stayed silent. Here was Emma, who at school had not liked one of his stories. Here was Gary, who had begun the evening cheerfully but now seemed rather defensive. Here was Jane, who perhaps had been on his side (if this was about sides) at school, but that was a long time ago. There was no Jennifer Loss, no Rex English, no Issie. He felt nervous again. He was not sure he knew who these people were now. Nine years is a long time.

But the suggestion from Jane had a hint of command in it.

"Come on, Mr Lind," urged Emma.

As so often in the past, Mark hesitated. "What sort of story?" he asked. His question was met with smiles and shrugs. He knew it was up to him.

"It had been a bright morning. That much, Simon Bradley could remember. And he knew he had gone to town in a

group – perhaps five or six of them? They were in their late teens and full of life. A vibrant summer day.

He was an old man now. He picked up his mug of coffee. He did not drink from it. He simply held it, as if that small embrace, the warmth through his fingers, could bring a fuller picture back to mind.

It was sometime in the holidays. Had they met at the bus station? They had danced – they couldn't really have danced? – through the streets. Had he fallen for Rachel before that morning? Whether he had or not, that was the day when it all went cascading through him. There had been no mention to her, of course, and she had said nothing. But sometimes he had wondered if she knew.

The group went into several shops, anywhere that caught their eye. And in a music shop Simon had seen a piano score of Pachelbel's Canon.

"I like this, I've always liked this, I wouldn't be able to play it."

The others had crowded round, Simon had taken it from the rack and bought it. The shop assistant had smiled but looked slightly relieved when the joyous group spilled back out on to the pavement.

He could not remember much else. Was there a milkshake somewhere? He had spent the next few weeks clumsily circling Rachel but nothing had happened. The autumn term began and school life returned.

It was a long time ago. Funny how he could remember the feel of that morning so clearly. And somewhere, surely, he still had the copy of Pachelbel's Canon? Or had it been thrown away when he moved into the home? It must have been. Or had he given it to someone? So much had gone.

He had taken it to school the next term. The piano teacher had been rather uncertain.

"It is very good, very good indeed, that you are beginning to buy your own pieces, building up your library, your repertoire. Perhaps I would not have suggested starting with the Pachelbel. A trifle overused, dare I say, but also, to be honest, some sections will be too difficult."

Simon tried the first two lines ("Slower, slower – otherwise it does get so, so fast later on"). And then his attention was turned to a new exam piece. Simon dutifully began to do battle and the Pachelbel was put to one side.

A year later his mother drove him to university. He was a little sad and scared to be moving away from home. Halfway through the first term there was a party. He found himself in a circle next to a new friend, Paul. There was a pause in the conversation.

"Live music," said Paul. "That's what we need. There's a piano over there. Si, you play, don't you?' Simon was caught off-balance. He meant to say no but hesitated too long. Well, why not? He then thought. "Yes, I can play, I'll get some music." He returned his room, rummaged in the cupboard and found the Pachelbel. He would only play the easy section, perhaps twice.

Back in the recreation room Paul shouted above the party noise. "Shut up for a bit. Simon wants to play the piano." Eventually there was quiet and Simon began to play. He thought he was going to play well but the fingers were not moving as they should. Too many notes were missed in the slow section. He played too quickly as he approached the fast section. He stopped, then crashed his hands down into an attempt at a chord.

73

"The Finale!" he called out. There was a brief silence then a few people clapped. Probably worse than if no one had clapped, thought Simon. Or he should just have tried 'Twinkle, Twinkle, Little Star'. At least he could play that, or once he could have done. Maybe he could not play anything now. This was his special piece, and he had spoiled it.

Towards the end of the term he met Helen. One evening when they were in the college music room, Simon sat at the piano and started to pick out the Pachelbel notes. "Do you like that, too?" asked Helen. "It is one of my favourites." She waited for Simon to pause and then said, slightly impatiently: "Here, let me have a go." And she sat down, and played the whole piece really well. "If ever we have musical evenings, best leave the playing to me." She laughed. He smiled wanly back.

The relationship did not last very long. After university Simon got a job not far from home. He settled into a new routine, and then one day he bumped into Rachel. They agreed to meet. She was living with her parents and Simon went round for a chat. He was slightly nervous; would she mention, or laugh at him, or be cross with him, for his clumsiness as a teenager all those summers ago?

There, on a piano, was a copy of Pachelbel's Canon. "Are you playing that?" he asked.

"I'm trying to, but I'm struggling. I'm working on the left hand," she replied.

"I've always struggled, too. But I'll have a go at the right hand." So they sat, and played. It was not very fluent and there was laughter and re-starts and uncertain timings. When one found it difficult, the other slowed down. There were moments when it really didn't sound too bad at all.

And they got to the end. "It's the first time that I've properly finished." said Simon. "I really enjoyed that."

Simon Bradley continued to hold the mug. As he stared at it the old eyes found it fuzzy round the edges. But he could remember so, so clearly the music, the moments, the humiliations and the joys, and Rachel.

"Mr Lind…" began Emma.

"Can we manage Mark? I am no longer your teacher."

"Mark," said Emma, hesitantly, "that was not what I was expecting. Do you tell different kinds of stories now? Does it depend where you are?"

"I don't know," said Mark. "It wasn't about anyone in particular. Perhaps it was just a story."

"I didn't understand the part near the start when he is holding the coffee and remembering the morning," said Jane "Is the whole thing a series of flashbacks?"

"Yes, he is in a residential home. Someone has just put Pachelbel's Canon on the music system and then all these memories come back. Sorry, I should have made that clear."

"That's an interesting thought, maybe we could talk about that," said Jane. "If there were one piece of music, that we, once we are in an old people's home, would want to hear and would bring back memories, what would it be?"

"Would want to hear, would bring back memories. Are they sometimes not two different things? And, while I am in the correcting mood," said Jennifer Loss, standing smiling in the doorway, "nothing, Mark, is just a story, you of all people should know that. We may not know what is in the story that matters to someone else, but somewhere, somehow, it counts. Always. Oh, and I'm sorry I am late."

Chapter 14: Preparing the ground

The next day, the new day, began.

Jenny had been welcomed. Mark had relaxed a little, it would be easier now that a former colleague had arrived. It changed the feel of the reunion. It both raised expectations and was a reminder of familiar ground. As he considered this, it dawned on him that he had never quite understood her role. What was she there to do?

"You are here," Gary addressed her over breakfast. "Does that mean that Issie might appear? And Mr English too? Mr Moore, the whole lot?"

"That is not for me to say," she replied. "And, in truth, I do not know."

"What do we do while we wait?" Mark asked.

"Hold on a moment," said Jane. "Let's get as clear as we can, even if that isn't very far. Miss Loss – or are you to be Jennifer, like Mr Lind is now Mark? – why are you here?"

"I am happy to be Jenny now. And I am here because I received a message."

"Who from, what did it say?" asked Gary.

"Nothing specific. Too vague to articulate. But here I am."

There was a slight silence.

"Have you ever heard about the imaginary pocket?" said Jenny.

"What's that?" asked Emma.

"Each one of us has an imaginary pocket. We take it in turns to suggest what can be put in the pocket. For example, I might suggest we put in our favourite memory from last year, or the place we might most like to visit, or our favourite colour, or anything really."

"Sounds somewhat bizarre and contrived to me," said Gary. "I'm not very comfortable with this sort of thing."

"Why a pocket?" asked Jane.

"So it stays with us, full of thoughts that can comfort, challenge or remind us. Think of how many good things you have heard and then forgotten. The imaginary pocket is a small memory trick to help us keep some of them."

The group agreed to try it after breakfast, with some reluctance but slightly relieved that some sort of activity had been suggested.

"Mark, you begin," Jenny said.

"I'm not sure where to start. You mentioned favourite colours? Let's do those, and we have to include an adjective. For me, I am going to say quiet purple."

"Misty grey," said Jane.

"Sunrise yellow," said Emma.

"Deep forest green" said Gary. "Sorry, that's two adjectives, unless we count forest green as a colour in its own right."

Jenny looked at him for a moment and then said, "For me, refreshing blue."

"That felt strange," commented Emma. "I wanted to be able to say why I chose the colour."

"How about five things people are frightened of?" Jenny suggested. "It doesn't have to be personal, just general."

"Fear of missing out," said Jane. "Just think of the number of adverts that use fear as motivation. You are being left behind, you are missing opportunities. You are this or that or the other; whatever you are, you are never quite what the advertisers suggest you should be."

"Should there be something there about fear of what other people think of us?" asked Emma.

"Does that depend on who those 'other people' are?" asked Jenny. "And why we have chosen their voices to be the ones we listen to?"

"Can I put in fear of having made the wrong decision?" Gary asked. "And then being haunted by past mistakes or uncertainties – 'what if I had gone the other route' and so on."

Mark leaned forward: "That's the key thing – uncertainty. If we knew absolutely what we are facing, or what we had got wrong, or whether we do have something to show for what we have done, or not, then perhaps we would not be so afraid? But we do not know how much pain there will be, so we do not know how to prepare. We do not know where the other path would have led so we cannot properly compare. It is the not knowing that churns us up. It is not the crisis itself but whether we can cope with the crisis. It is that uncertainty that can be so difficult to live with."

"Perhaps the uncertainty itself needs to be named and faced, as much as the possible crisis itself," said Jenny.

"Fear of someone leaving us," said Emma, rather abruptly. "Then realising that life is fragile and then being over-cautious about getting anything and everything wrong."

Mark broke the ensuing silence: "That one seemed to move on quite quickly. Let's put something else into the imaginary pocket. How about favourite times of the year? I always liked Christmas. Everyone in a good mood. The familiar decorations being brought out. Always the same but always new; the sense that this was when home really felt like home. And I always love hearing, or reading, or seeing, 'A Christmas Carol'. I like the trick of letting a character revisit his past in order to make sense of the present. Wouldn't we all like to do that?"

"Scrooge had the ghosts to help him," said Jenny. "We can't always be sure we will look back so accurately."

Gary said: "When I was a child, it was the first day of the summer holidays. Waking up, seeing the light come past the edge of the curtains but knowing that I did not have to get up, that there was no school for weeks and weeks." He smiled broadly, and said half-dramatically, half-wistfully: "Freedom stretching in front of me…"

Emma broke in: "The holidays for me meant confusion and edginess. At school I knew where I was and what I was meant to be doing. I felt I belonged. Whether holidays were happy depended on whether my parents had made sensible arrangements or not. They often had not, or they had made arrangements that I did not like. If there was still tension about when I was staying with whom, or who was spending more money on trips, then the whole thing could become a nightmare. To be honest, Christmas was not much better. In fact, it was usually worse.

"I don't want to discuss it," she continued. "I just needed to say it. Jane, your turn now."

"This will sound a bit banal, and I know I am not quite answering the question," said Jane. "But for me a special memory was the first time I bought a coffee on the train. We didn't have much money when I was young. Buying anything on the train seemed a luxury, out of our reach. A train ride was a treat in itself. To buy anything from the trolley was only what rich people did. If we ever went on a train we would always have taken our own cartons of juice. I can now buy a cup of coffee on the train (not that I often do). That became a symbol for me."

"For me," said Jenny simply, "it is the changes of the seasons, so I get four each year."

"Shall we leave the pocket thing for the moment?" said Jane. "Mark, did you ever tell any more stories about the knight in the castle?"

"No, I stopped when I left St. George's."

Gary broke in "What was that about? I must have missed that, or forgotten it. Is this a real knights in armour story, swords and castles and that sort of thing? What is he going to fight? Soldiers of a neighbouring evil baron? A dragon?"

Mark shrugged, with a smile: "No need to go back to that now."

But Jenny interrupted: "Gather round, gather round," she said in a stage whisper. "Let the storyteller weave his spell. Step up, Mark Lind."

Mark told the story again. Sir Richard, Catherine, the approaching threat. The winter meeting in the church.

81

"What happens next? Does he fight or not?" exclaimed Gary when Mark had finished. "You can't leave it there. I want the trumpets and the horses, the skirmishes and one big victorious, resolving, battle."

"You never said why the bad baron was grabbing the land;" said Jane. "Can you fill in that gap? Or was it simply greed?"

Mark smiled. "I feel rather out of practice and rather rusty. But here goes."

Sir Richard thought he knew why Sir Adam was trying to grow his power and his control. Sir Adam's father had given land to his four children. These were large and good territories, filled with fruitful farms and well-stocked woods. The two sons and two daughters were rich and had all they needed. But Adam had not found it easy to be on the same level as his brother and sisters, and sometimes wondered if their land was more productive than his. He had enough, but enough did not satisfy. He was deeply competitive. Hence his thoughts had turned to expansion and conquest.

"So he has enough but wants more?" asked Catherine. "Simply so he can have more than the others?"

"Or, and this is perhaps a stronger motive, so that he will be seen to have more than the others. That is important to him."

"And that is all it is? That little cause to cause so much pain?"

"What else could it be? He has all he needs." Sir Richard paused. "It may be a small cause, but once it is rooted in someone like Adam, it is hard to dislodge."

82

"Do you tell stories often now?" asked Emma.

"Not so often. When I was at St. George's I had permission to do so. Rightly or wrongly, that helps. Although occasionally I feel I should tell one whether I am asked to or not."

"As you did with a poem all those years ago," said Jenny.

"The one in Ed's lunchtime meeting? I still don't know if I was right to do that. But I have been thinking about what you said last night about stories. I think you are right. Storytellers do not feel fully in control of what they are saying, or why they are saying it. It is as if I am simply catching hold of a glimpse of something that is already there. I am sharing, not creating."

Emma looked as if she was about to speak. She then shook her head.

"Emma?" queried Jane, very gently.

"I feel I would like to try a poem that has been on my mind since yesterday morning. Would you all mind very much? I know I am not a real STAP, Storyteller and Poet – we never thought of a better name, did we? – like Mr Lind."

"Of course we would not mind," said Jane encouragingly.

"Thank you. Here it is."

Night slowly fades
As lightening dawn
colours through the world
and me.
I had thought to take the final road
from all uncertainty.
But knowing, seeing, naming, loving
has held me safe
for one more day.

In the silence that followed, a voice quietly said: "Emma, may I ask: why were you so unhappy?"

"That is a very brave question, Jane," Emma said, and it was difficult to know whether there was a smile or a challenge in her voice. But she then looked away from the group and said quietly: "Let me tell you what really hurts a child when their parents split up. Or at least this was how it was for me, I don't know if it is the same for everyone. It is the feeling that I was not good enough to hold them to stay together. Or that my love was not good enough. He told me that it was simply an issue between him and mum and all would be well in the end. But that is not how it feels to a child, or at least not for me. Why did he no longer want, or be able, to be with me, with us? Why couldn't I fix it, like child heroes fix things in books? I understand it better now, of course, or at least I think I do. But at the time I simply thought I was not enough, that it was my fault. If I had been a better child, would it have happened? But I was young and I never articulated all this, even to myself. So, Jane, as you say, I was unhappy." Her voice hardened slightly. "I am sorry it was so noticeable."

She looked back at the circle of faces. "Don't ask me for any more."

"Emma," said Jane. "It was not very noticeable. I did not especially think of you as unhappy at the time. It was your poem that got me thinking, and then I blurted it out. Let's leave it there and do something else. And thank you for saying what you did."

"Before we move on," said Gary, "sorry to come back to this: Mr Lind, Mark, the story you told, the knight and the castle. You avoided the issue by going back and filling in another part of the background. But I want to know. You never finished it. Tell me, did he fight?"

Mark smiled. "You decide."

"No," Gary insisted, "I want to know. Did he put the armour back on? Did he march out one last time? Were the troops rallied and the swords sharpened? Did he do what deep down he knew he had to do?"

"He did. He rode again. Facing what needed to be faced. One more time."

Gary leaned back and closed his eyes.

And they heard the front door close, and footsteps in the hall.

Framed in the doorway to the sitting room was the half-forgotten but immediately recognisable figure of Rex English.

Chapter 15: The quest is renewed

"Good morning, everyone. Thank you for being here."

They had stood to greet him but there was no rushing forward. He stepped forward and joined the circle.

"My thanks to you all. You arrived here not understanding the invitation. You have given time to each other and have shared something of yourselves. Sometimes a chapter is needed when the focus needs to be on one character beginning to move to a different place, four of you have done that for the fifth this morning. There will have been benefit to the other four; that is how it always works, we cannot help someone without being helped ourselves. And some of us have indeed moved far this morning. But it is the fifth who has moved furthest, who is now beginning to return. It will also, if I may add, have made a considerable difference to the sixth, even though she is not here."

He ignored their questioning glances.

"There is now a journey to make. Are we ready for a short walk?"

There was a flurry of activity as coats were found.

In the porch, Emma asked, "Where are we going?"

"We are going to continue the quest we were part of all those years ago and it would be good if we went quickly. We are going west. There is someone we are likely to meet on the way and I want you to see him while he is still there."

"This feels different, more urgent," said Jane. "Has something happened? Are we in danger? Is this an adventure?" And Mark saw a glimpse of the excited teenager that he had met all those years ago.

"No more than normal. There is always danger, Jane. The world is not a safe place; did you ever think it was? It is always an adventure. There is always possible danger to emotions or values, danger to relationships, dangers to our hopes and dreams, dangers to how we see the world. Very occasionally physical danger, but that is seldom the worst kind."

Mr English did not lead them to the front gate. Instead they went round the house, into the back garden, through a narrow gate and into the woods. "Not one for small talk, is he?" whispered Emma to Gary, "even after nine years. That sounded like a speech in there." But Gary only responded with a nod and a quick smile, and then focused again on the path into the deepening forest.

 They walked for about an hour and then reached the edge of a clearing.

"Stay close to me," Mr English said and the group gathered behind him.

Nothing happened. They gazed across and around the clearing. Perhaps we have missed something, thought Mark, perhaps we are too late for whatever it is, perhaps it was never here. And then a voice rang out.

"So, Arthur, you are here."

"Of course. Would you expect anything different?" Rex English replied. "I like to see how you choose to appear in each age."

"And what name do you give to me this time?" Stepping half out of the shadows on the other side of the clearing was a smartly dressed man – mid-thirties, thought Mark, but in the dappled light it was difficult to judge.

"I do not yet know the name you presently give yourself, but I know that the Morgan Le Fay blood still runs through you. I know of your mentoring of Ed Moore. And I know what you seek."

The man stayed where he was, on the other side of the clearing.

"Why did you bring these five with you?"

"I always travel with others, you know that. You travel alone. You like to sit on a throne set apart from others. I sit at a round table. We are different in that way. And I wanted my friends to see you, to know that you exist."

"Oh yes, I exist," the man replied. "And I know how to lead, and you do not. We can ignore that now, let me get to the point. Since these five are here I have gifts for them. Seven gifts in fact. More than enough for one each. After all, these are gifts that some of them deeply desire and they may wish to have as many as they can. May they not hear about them?"

"They have been told about them, and they have been told about the better seven."

"Ah, but that was a long time ago, dear Arthur. And, despite your arrogance, it is possible that not everyone hangs on your every word. And even if they did, I think some may have forgotten. In fact, looking at their lives, I know that some have indeed forgotten your little speeches and have already shown a particular interest in these gifts. And no doubt when you struggled to explain them all those years ago you put your own biased twist on the seven. In the interests of fairness should they not hear my interpretation?"

Mr English smiled. "Your interest in fairness is somewhat out of character."

"In a nutshell, my friends," the man called out across the clearing, "what I offer you means that you can do all that you want to do. Would you like to hear more?"

Mr English broke in: "What you offer leads to loneliness, entrapment, deceit and regret. It does not lead to what people really want. It would be surprising if they did, since you do not truly understand their deep desires."

"You are tiresome and rude and tend to interrupt," said the man. "Let me speak to them."

"You constantly speak to them, peddling your lies of dissatisfaction through a multiplicity of other voices. This time you are out in the open, this time you must deal with me. And what you offer cannot truly be called 'gifts'. Whoever receives them pays a high price."

"Some observations, Arthur, to shake your complacency. I see that you are six, not seven. I look and I count and I see a dwindling band, you are incomplete. Your precious table will be a lonely place before long. I offer pleasure for now, for today. Your strategy is to pretend there is a distant tomorrow, talking falsely of unseen hope and meaning and purpose, as if there is anything more than what we can see and touch. I look for hard proof away from myths and feelings. And all the time your precious group is fading. Today you are six. Tomorrow it may be five. You know as well as I do that something has gone wrong. What is it?"

Mr English smiled. "It is not what you hope, and in truth this particular wrong will be healed, is indeed already being healed. And do you think for one moment that I would tell you what it is?" He turned back into the woods, beckoning the others to follow. As they did, Mark looked back, and saw their adversary still standing on his edge of the clearing. His arms were folded, and he was watching.

The group kept walking. The pace slowed. A halt was called and they sat in a circle.

"What was that all about?" Emma asked.

"He is intrigued and threatened because we have one here who long ago said that he wants to find the Grail, and that always troubles him. Because we have one here who has been willing to be a Merlin. Because we have one who has shown courage in great suffering and who has begun to tell poems herself, perhaps becoming another Merlin. Because there is one who patiently struggles through each day, not quite feeling she is at peace, not quite confident in herself and her resources, but who has a profound quality of perseverance. Jennifer and me he knows well. He knows that one of this group is missing and if there is restoration then we will be seven again. He wants to know how much of a threat we are. Is he only yet again fighting against ridiculed, old and complex Rex English, or are there others on my side? Are the seats at the table to be filled again?

"He seeks always to distract. He feels threatened because (somewhat to his surprise) he finds that he has to fight me afresh in every generation. He pretends that nothing matters but it matters deeply to him whether people think as he does and he is fearful when they do not. Sometimes he seeks to distract by persuading people to spend themselves on what they do not really want. He tells them that the grass is greener elsewhere but does not tell them that it is artificial grass. He tells them to chase targets that

90

do not matter, to tick boxes that do not exist. He wants truth to be very narrow and to be determined by the limits of his impoverished imagination. He wants us to believe that the wisdom of history and the experience of humanity is to be mocked or ignored. He pretends he follows no external reference points but he does in fact believe in an absolute guide, and this guide is what he himself thinks best. No wonder he is angry and frustrated. Despite all his best efforts, the round table is never finally destroyed."

"And why did we have to see him?" asked Mark.

"To be reminded that there is a real foe and a real battle. But be on your guard, he does not always look like that. He changes appearance to fit his context.

"My battle with him, and his like, continues through the ages. You need to be watching for yourselves in this day, the day that you are given. Be on your guard. He plays to win. Whatever it takes to detach you from your quest, he will seek to do."

"Are we on a quest now?" asked Jane.

"You have always been on a quest, dear Jane," Mr English smiled, "and, my friend, you need to learn to enjoy it more and to know that you are a central part of it. You are not on the margins. You matter and you are needed. You are central to more stories than you realise.

"We must start walking again. Westwards. It is about five miles from here."

"What is?" asked Gary, speaking for the first time since they had left the clearing.

"Glastonbury."

Chapter 16: A forest, a meal and a story

The six walked steadily, following winding paths through overhanging branches, their eyes lost in the deep greens of the trees and shadows as they looked around them.

"I had not realised there was such a forest outside Glastonbury," said Jane.

"Sometimes there is," said Mr English, simply.

Mark stopped. His mind raced as he tried to control what this answer might mean. Where is this leading? Who really is this person? Why is there so little I understand? Would life ever return to normal? And, in a very prosaic moment, a sudden fleeting question as to whether he had been wise to read the job vacancies in the library all those Fridays ago.

Rex English turned and smiled at him. "I told you it was an adventure and that the journey is dangerous. But don't worry, good storyteller, all will be well."

Jenny leaned forward and quoted:

In forest paths we're found and lost
And lives are turned and veils grow thin.
And worlds collide and plays entwine
In mixed and magic, dangerous dark.

She went on: "Do you remember that one, Mark? You touched on something important then, so important that I closed that part of the lesson down quickly. I was not sure where it might be heading. And remember this morning, remember the colours people chose."

It became quiet again. The group continued walking. The path began to wind upwards and they reached the top of a low hill. The trees had thinned and they could look across to Glastonbury.

"Now, let us sit for a moment. We are probably all feeling a little hungry." Rex English put down his bag and brought out some bread rolls. He passed them round. "Is anyone thirsty?" And he brought out a bottle and a wooden cup. "I have only got one, we will have to share."

They ate and drank together.

"I think we have time for a story." He leaned back contentedly "We should always have a story with a meal."

"Mark," said Jane. "For old time's sake, can you tell us more about the knight?" There were nods of encouragement and Mark began.

It had been a brief but bloody battle. Sir Adam's forces had been defeated. He agreed to meet Sir Richard to discuss his departure from the land.

But when they met it seemed that Sir Adam had changed his mind.

"You see," he said, waving towards a group of men on horseback. "I still have enough of an army to cause you damage if need be. These soldiers trust me. And I see no reason to leave."

"You say they trust you, but what do they trust you to do for them? To lead them to defeat again?" asked Sir Richard.

"To act in their interests. To give them land. You may have won that little skirmish, but I have enough strength to fight on."

"All you will have done is show them that violence is an unpredictable weapon. And if you had won they know that anything you give to them will have been stolen from others. They will wonder if one day you may steal from them. Or they may follow your example and steal from you. Are they trusting you wisely? Are you wise to trust them? All you are doing today is showing that you can break a promise. Any fool can do that. I have defeated you once, I can go on doing so. It is time to stop, Adam, it is time to see how things are. I am strong, much stronger, than you realise. Be content with what you were given by your father. Make peace with your brother and sisters. Go home."

The two knights were on horseback, facing each other in the middle of a field. Sir Adam gestured, some of his men kicked their horses into a trot and drew near to Sir Richard.

"You said this would be a peaceful meeting," said Sir Richard, calmly.

"As you say, you always have to ask what trusting someone really means," Sir Adam said, contemptuously. "What do you trust someone like me to do? You are not just going to walk through them this time. They have their orders." He backed his horse away.

The soldiers surged forward. In a moment Sir Richard would be surrounded but he spurred his horse forward and rode directly at his foe, moving so fast that Sir Adam's men could only hurriedly strike with glancing blows as he passed between them like the wind. He reached Sir Adam with sword outstretched. Sir Adam parried the blow and at

94

the same time lunged forward with his heavy shield, seeking to unseat or at least unbalance him. But Sir Richard was now moving very quickly, dropping his sword and grabbing the top of Sir Adam's shield with both hands. He forced the shield down and, in doing so, began to topple his adversary from the saddle. Sir Adam swung his sword and tried to strike, but by then the downward momentum dragged him to the ground and the blow never found its mark.

There was a roar of voices and the sound of galloping hooves. Sir Adam's men turned to see Sir Richard's soldiers surrounding them in turn. They lowered their swords.

Sir Richard turned and faced them. "It is time for you to go. And take him with you."

"He does not belong to us," one of them said. "He can look after himself." And they turned their horses and rode back towards the mountains.

Sir Richard acknowledged his soldiers and rode slowly back with them towards his castle. Some of the blows had found their mark, glancing though they had been. The bruises would grow more painful in the coming days.

But he was heading for home.

Mark looked up. "Is it enough?"

"It is enough," said Mr English. "And, amongst other things, we may wish to note the first letters of the last three words of the story and remember a room and a candle, a poem and a winter's afternoon. Thank you, Mark Lind."

He looked round. "I will leave you now. If you want to visit Glastonbury, it is easy to reach from here. If you want to return to the cottage, the path leads straight back."

Chapter 17: Words of healing, words of hope

It was three weeks later.

"You don't have to worry. I have changed my mind."

Isobel looked at the message. She did not believe it. She had grown so accustomed to tension and fear in the last six months. When was he going to begin? Would he pounce and shred her reputation or would it be a drip-feed of quiet words to friends and colleagues?

"You don't have to worry. I have changed my mind."

And now it might not happen at all.

Unless this was a game he was playing. She did not trust him.

Again she turned it all over in her mind. What she had done as a teenager, or, as she increasingly wondered, what had been done to her. It sometimes made her wryly smile when she remembered that while everyone else was fussing about a change of Headmaster and staff she was increasingly preoccupied in her own private world of confusion and pain. Nothing else had felt as if it had mattered. She had nearly talked to Mr Lind but had decided against doing so. (What use was he, anyway, he was only a storyteller, although she had been quite fond of him.)

But then a few weeks later she had rashly told Gary in a moment when her guard was down, a conversation she had then immediately deeply regretted. And now she faced the recent, unexpected renewed contact, gently threatening

97

that the past could be brought noisily into the present. She had repeatedly asked herself what would happen if people knew. Would they understand that the world looks very different when you are sixteen? Or would they judge and always associate her name with what had happened? And why, oh why, had she on that vivid Saturday night, told him? What had made her think he could trust him? The circular thoughts began again and again, even while the words of the message, which might, just might, break the circle, remained somewhere in her mind.

She did not trust him.

She decided to go out. Perhaps the fresh bright air would give weight or clarity to the hint of relief that these words might yet bring. Perhaps they might begin to seem true, after all.

She had not gone to the reunion. How could she have done?

She went to the park and looked for an empty bench. But her favourite ones by the pond were occupied. She gave up the search and walked back to the first one she had passed and sat in attempted solitude at one end. The other occupant was buried in a newspaper and looked unlikely to disturb anyone. She closed her eyes.

"You have done well."

She struggled to place the voice among the distant memories in her mind. She opened her eyes and glanced at her neighbour on the bench. Mr English had put down his paper and was looking at her steadily.

"You have done well," he repeated.

Isobel was silent for a moment. She had not seen her former Headmaster for nine years. She quietly, firmly, said:

"No I haven't."

A flicker of a smile crossed his face. "I think I am a better judge of that than you are." He reached across and touched her hand. "Issie, it is going to be all right." He then leaned back, clasped his hands behind his head and began to speak.

"For the past six months you have lived with the fear of an old secret being revealed and the fear of your reputation being ruined. You have been frightened of the reaction and the hurt that others would feel if they knew. You have felt trapped and uncertain and no outcome looked a good one. But in those six months you have kept going. Each day, summoning up the courage to go to work; each day, trying to treat others well despite the turmoil inside you; each day, holding on. I say that you have done well. Your determination to hold on, however fragile that determination may have seemed to you, and to do what is right while wondering if your world would collapse, is much more important in my eyes than the imagined or real effects if the news had become public. You have done well.

"And now you have heard that the threat has been lifted, that the past will not become public. I am here to tell you that the message was genuine. Gary means it. He has changed his mind. Or, to be accurate, he has changed that part of his mind which had become corrupted. He has traded it in for a better model. He has won his battle. He is back on the real quest. He will blackmail you no more. He will not carry out his plans. You are free."

Issie looked up and said rather coldly, "I find it difficult to believe."

"You don't have to believe *it*, you have to believe *me*. And I am telling the truth. The burden is taken away."

"But he may change his mind again."

"He will not. He now knows that his threat was a burden for him as well as for you. In setting you free he has been set free himself. He understands that. He does not want the burden again."

Issie hesitated. "If, if, if this is true then I might begin to feel free, or begin to imagine myself feeling free. I can see that. And I will be so glad and relieved, more than words can say. But it is difficult to accept. And there is something more. I not only felt trapped, I felt very sad. I had thought Gary was my friend. His threats have upset me as well as scared me."

"He understands that, too. He is deeply sorry. You may perhaps one day want to forgive him and it may be good to meet."

"I think I will want to forgive. I am not sure I am ready to meet him yet, but I do want to forgive. I know that will be part of what I have to do. A quest, even." She looked up and smiled.

"Dearest Issie. There, you speak like a true knight of the table. Most people would only have got to the point of 'wanting to want to forgive'. You are already a step ahead." Rex English stood up. "I always knew you were a good choice. I hope we shall meet again soon."

***

Jane and Gary faced each other over a table in a café.

"Thank you for this," said Gary. "It is good to see an old friend again."

"I was sorry to hear you had lost your job. I enjoyed seeing you at the weekend and so it seemed right to be in touch once I heard the news. Do you want to say what happened?"

Gary shrugged. "I was going to be part of a big project, but changed my mind."
`
"Did Glastonbury have something to do with it?"

Gary paused. "Well, I might as well tell you something of it. Just between ourselves?"

"Of course."

"A few months ago Mr Moore contacted me about a scheme. He remembered me from school and seemed to think that I might be of some use, being an apparently popular music journalist. There was serious money behind an idea to set up some specialist colleges to train teachers or tutors or lecturers, or something like that, who would then work across the country with thousands of performing arts students. As I say, the money was big. If I'd helped, it would have done me no harm at all. I would have had a share.

"Those behind the colleges would have a significant amount of influence over the sort of people who would be training the stars of the future. There was then a plan to roll out similar colleges for journalists. Imagine the quiet influence and power you could have over society. There was part of me that became unsure about the motives and I heard whispers of financial links with various businesses.

If leading celebrities and media personalities had unconsciously taken on certain philosophies and attitudes, then you could have considerable control over the culture and values of a generation, including banal but lucrative things like shopping habits and viewing habits, and even of how tolerant they are of different views to their own. I occasionally wondered if this was a moral as well as a career choice, but I must admit I became very good at squashing my conscience."

"And what did Glastonbury have to do with it?"

"The man we met in the glade. I was sure I had heard his voice before but I couldn't place it. Then I realised that someone in the group who approached me had sounded rather like him. As we walked on through that forest the need to make a choice became clear. Quite simply, I realised I did not trust the voice of the man in the clearing. And then Mr Lind's final story got me thinking about trust. What do I really trust people to do? I was also moved, very moved, by Emma's honesty earlier in the day. I wondered if I could ever be so honest about my feelings or motives. And her words reminded me that people can get very hurt. There is someone I would have badly hurt if I had made the wrong decision. The scheme that had seemed attractive and dazzling and flattering seemed increasingly manipulative and murky. So I had to say no."

"It was a brave decision to say no. I am sure people will respect your integrity."

Gary laughed. "I appreciate the thought, but my world does not work like that. Not by these people it wasn't – respect and integrity are not linked in their vocabulary. They put pressure on my present employers, who quickly got rid of me. They spread rumours that I was finished or uninterested or lazy. People look down on me now (I can sense it) with a mixture of sorrow and contempt. I have lost a lot in the past three weeks."

Jane looked at her coffee. And then softly asked: "Who was the person you didn't want to hurt? Was it Issie?"

There was a long pause.

"Yes. Her father is a government adviser. In fact he is a very influential one. With him on side, it could all have happened. Without him, it may well not. I was asked to pressure Issie to help. I think that might have been why she wasn't with us that weekend. I realised I was being unfair on her. So I stopped my pressure on her. I'd rather not say more about that and please don't tell her I have said any of this." He paused. "How did you know it was about her?"

"She never told me any details but her moving out of our little group at school seemed odd at the time. After Mr English and Mr Lind left I thought we would become closer but I sensed something had happened that was separating us. We had been good friends but there was suddenly a barrier, and a part of her that I wasn't allowed to know about. And I knew she thought about telling Mr Lind but never did, so I wondered if something serious was on her mind. And when she didn't come to the reunion I wondered if there was an old hurt still being felt. Forgive me for being blunt when I say this: I didn't think that I or Emma was the cause of that, so I wondered if in some way it might have been you. Sorry."

Gary nodded and looked down.

"You guessed right."

Jane paused. "What will you do now?" she asked.

"I'll wait and see, but I feel I have won a battle that I needed to win and so I am feeling positive, even if my job prospects are looking rather weak. Let's leave it there now, but thank you for being willing to listen. That's enough about me. Tell me how things are with you."

"This will sound very small in comparison, but the reunion reminded me that I had been part of the appointment of Mr Lind. It then made me begin to wonder if my role at various moments in my life has been bigger than I thought it was. I wondered if I had got rather narrow in my view of what I could do. I will never have much confidence in myself but perhaps I can have more confidence in what I can do, in what I can contribute. I don't know what that will mean but somehow life seems to have the possibility of being more vibrant, of the painting becoming brighter. Misty grey can be attractive but there are other colours I could be free to use as well."

Chapter 18: Endings and beginnings

Mark was in the library and the familiar table on the first floor was still there. It had seemed good to remember he had this place to come back to, although he was not quite sure why. After that strange term nine years ago he had continued to be on the supply lists for various schools, but he knew that his quick departure from St. George's did not look impressive in the 'previous experience' column of application forms, nor did the unusual job title. His mind went back to the very first comment at his interview. Perhaps Mr English had been wrong, perhaps there were many poets and storytellers, perhaps they simply did not want to admit it. So he had avoided the library for many years and looked at lists of vacancies elsewhere, but the reunion had made him wonder what it would like to be back and so he had returned.

There was nothing on the desk in front of him, no vacancies pages open. He sat quietly, remembering and reflecting. He looked up at a slight noise and there was Rex English sitting down opposite him. With him was Emma.

"Are you glad you said yes?" Mr English asked, without preamble. "To the advertisement, all those years ago?"

"I was just thinking of that," said Mark with a wry smile. "Yes, I am glad. I feel I was briefly caught up in a world I never knew existed. It has been exciting, confusing and uncertain and there is so much I don't understand. But it was a glimpse that I am glad I have had. And I am still trying to work out what that Glastonbury visit was all about."

"You have not only glimpsed into the world you mention, you have become part of it. You are the storyteller and poet. I always have to have at least one at the table."

"But I am not a good one. Can't you see that? My poems are boring or trite and I don't tell stories well."

"The word 'good' was not mentioned in the advertisement. I wanted you. The quality of what you did was of less importance than the quality of what motivated you."

"That is why I came back that morning all those years ago," Emma interjected. "You may have unknowingly been tactless with the story, and it felt rather cosy and predictable, but I sensed you were safe, and that you meant well. That counts for a lot."

"There," laughed Rex English. "You can always rely on Emma to be honest."

"I know," says Mark, "and that means the encouragement counts all the more." He stared intently at the table and then looked up. "I will keep on trying to be your storyteller and poet."

"Thank you," said Rex English. "And well done. Remember the Alfred poem you told in your first lesson. Keep going, Mark, keep going."

Emma turned to him. "Is this the end?"

"No. The end is far off and the journey is long and we have many different battles ahead. Whether we will fight together or separately is not for us to decide. But the seven have become complete again." He paused and then said: "Well, noble heroine, has the dawn continued to grow?"

"The piano story that Mark told. I began to realise that I did not have to do everything to perfection on my own. And then the reminder of the seven deadly foes or whatever we are calling them – I realised that I had been hurt badly by people who had been trapped by some of these. That made it easier to see things clearly. It is easier to begin to forgive when you are honest about what someone has done and why they might have done it."

She stopped. And then said softly and slowly to Mr English, "You never gave up on me, did you?"

For the first time since they had met, Mark thought that Rex English was taken aback, as if he was not quite sure how to answer. He was looking at Emma. His eyes were glistening and seemed filled with poignancy and tiredness, richness, compassion and sacrifice. But there was a glint of satisfaction and even joy, as if vital words had been spoken. As if truth had been named.

"I don't give up. I make mistakes, lots of them. I have at times been careless or plain wrong. I am often misunderstood or misled. But I don't give up. And, dear Emma, you noticed. It is the one thing I can do. Despite everything. When all else fails. I don't give up."

His voice became more settled again: "And, Emma, I felt that you needed to know that somewhere there are candles still being properly made."

"There, Mr Lind," said Emma, turning to Mark with a smile. "Perhaps the story was not wasted after all."

Rex English smiled too. "*And so you help me, and perhaps I help you.*" Jennifer liked that poem, Mark. I think that you and Emma should meet and talk further."

"I was not very good all those years ago," said Mark. "Shall we try again?"

"Yes," said Emma.

***

The two old friends stood together, looking over the lake.

"Do you think it was a good chapter?" asked Jennifer.

"I think it was. But much will depend on how they begin the next one."

"You have answered about them, not about you. Was it a good chapter for you?"

"There were moments that felt positive, but I was ineffective with Ed Moore. I would have liked to have won him round, or at least help him begin to see there was more to life than he is fighting for. I was perhaps too direct. And sometimes I talk too much."

"Perhaps what you said, and what Mark said, will have sown seeds somewhere in him."

"Perhaps. We never fully know. You were a vital part of the chapter. Thank you for joining me for it."

"Of course I would join you," said Jennifer. "It is the least I can do. After all, despite everything I put you through, we have our poem.

The dreamy days, the lazy walks, the silent pacts to stay
The gentle light, the shining eyes, the words no need to say

"The silent pact still holds. Anyway, what would the others say if we sat around and did nothing?" and she laughed.

"Do you think of them often?"

"Of course. But no longer that those times made the only golden age. Each age can be golden. But there is a warmth in looking back and thinking about them, and what we did, and what it came to mean."

He smiled, "I think of them too. What would they make of us as school teachers?!"

He reached over and held her hand for a moment. "Thank you again, dear queen, once and future." She smiled, and then the smile became solemn as she slowly bowed her head to her king. She turned and began to walk away. Looking back she could see that he had stepped forward and was now sitting on a rock at the water's edge, gazing out over the lake. He could almost have been fishing.

"Until next time," she called out.

"As ever," he said and turned his gaze back to the water. "And thank you."

Lightning Source UK Ltd.
Milton Keynes UK
UKOW04f0948160915

258719UK00002B/10/P